This is dedicated to all the veterans who came home missing a piece of themselves.

Thank you for your service, your sacrifices, and may God bless and continue to watch over you.

CHAPTER

One

I shove two fingers between my collar and neck and tug hard as I stride through the revolving door of our newest hotel. This damn tie is strangling me. It's bad enough I have to make an appearance at these events, but Drew's insistence that I wear a suit and tie is pure torture for me and he knows it.

Fuck it. I grasp the knot of the tie, loosen it, and yank the noose-like silk over my head, shoving the offending article in my jacket pocket. I unbutton the top two buttons of my shirt as well, letting out a sigh of pleasure at the ability to breathe freely again.

What's Drew going to do, fire me? He can't. I own thirty percent of the company, just like him.

Just to really get under his skin, I stop at the coat check, swap my suit jacket for a ticket, and grin widely. I thank the attendant who has just unwittingly helped me to drag at least one eye roll out of my younger brother this evening.

Yep, Drew is my younger brother, but he does more to keep me on the straight and narrow than the other way around.

After spending seven years in the Army, three of those years deployed overseas for active duty, he understands that my edges will always be a little rough. But that doesn't stop him from trying to smooth them out when he can.

Strolling into the grand ballroom, I smile as a swell of pride courses through me. The latest hotel in our chain, Sapphire Resorts, has turned out beautifully, and without a doubt, I believe it's going to be a big success, especially with the location so central to the financial district.

When did I start caring so much about this shit? I chuckle softly with a small shake of my head and then look for the closest bar. I need a drink if I'm going to get through the next two hours.

I head to the back corner of the ballroom, a spot I know will most likely be a bit quieter, but pause when a flash of gold catches the corner of my eye. I turn my head and draw in a long, appreciative breath as I scan the beauty making her way across the room. Her gaze seems focused on the bar at the front of the room, so I turn my body and casually drift in that direction instead.

As I'm walking, I scan from her gold-clad toes, up her bare, toned legs to mid-thigh, where the hem of her sheer cream dress ends. The sheer fabric is scattered with a thousand different types of golden gemstones that hug her tiny waist and perfect breasts, reflecting against every light in the room.

But what really draws my attention is the open back of the dress. Her entire back is bare, exposing skin so smooth, it appears flawless. I clasp and unclasp my hand as I fight the urge to press it flat against her skin as I move closer. It's hard to tell if her hair is long or short because it's all piled on top of her head, as if she knows the power her exposed back possesses.

I stop several feet from the bar and watch as she attempts to cut a path through the mingling throng, waving to try to catch the bartender's attention. The bartender is female; otherwise, I'm certain she would have had a drink in front her before she lifted a single finger.

I continue watching until a rather stout gentleman slides up beside her and attempts to make conversation. It's amusing to watch her try to be kind to the man until I see him reach out and slide his pinky finger down her arm suggestively, a look of disgust crossing her face at the action.

Anger surges through my body, and within seconds, I'm pushing myself between her and the man. A warning snarl slips from my lips as I glare at him and place my hand flat against the center of her back. It feels like silk. It's the single thought that flies through my head before I smile down at her and brush a kiss against her cheek.

"Hello, darling. Are you having a problem getting the cocktails?"

Her wide blue eyes look up at me in surprise and then in knowing relief as she immediately plays into my little game. "Yes! Have you come to rescue me, babe?"

I can't help the wide grin that breaks across my face

when she gives me a small wink and mouths silently, "Thank you so much".

"I have." I give her my full attention for only a second, my gaze locking onto hers long enough to see light grey flecks mixed into the blue surrounding her pupil, reminding me of waves churning at sea.

I break contact and look at the bartender's name tag. "Excuse me, Greta?"

Whether it's because I'm a somewhat handsome male, or because she realizes a Sapphire is standing in front of her, suddenly, all of her attention is focused on me.

"Yes, sir, what can I get you?" Her cheeks turn a light pink as she fidgets with the bottle opener in her fingers.

I smile warmly to try to settle her nerves, nodding toward the back of the bar. "I'll have a couple fingers of that whiskey, please, on the rocks." I turn my head toward the vision in gold, locking eyes with hers again. "And, I'm sorry Darling, what did you want again?"

I watch as her eyes narrow, one side of her gloss-lined lips tilting up in a smirk as she tells the bartender that she'll have a Goose on the rocks, her eyes never leaving mine.

Greta sets our drinks down in front of us within seconds, then busies herself with the next person in line. I watch as her delicate fingers, tipped with nails painted black, wrap around the glass to raise it to her mouth, her lips kissing the edge as she draws in a small sip of the clear liquid before slowly lowering it.

"Thanks for rescuing me."

I look down in shock as the hand that was on her back is suddenly cold and empty. I watch her turn and walk away for only a second before I grab my whiskey off the bar and quickly follow, calling after her.

"I'm Ben, in case you were wondering."

She stops mid-stride, anchors her foot and then spins around, stopping in front of me, a cocky grin on her face.

"I wasn't. Wondering." She flashes a cocky grin and then continues, "But nice to meet you, Ben. Thanks again."

She raises the glass in salute and moves to turn again, but I take a step closer as she does, causing her to falter, one eyebrow raising in curiosity. "Yes?"

"You aren't going to tell me your name?" *Jesus, I sound like a desperate idiot who's never seen a beautiful woman before.*

She smirks and takes another sip from her glass, scanning me from head to toe then pausing briefly at what I'm sure are my tattoos peeking out of my open collar, and then shakes her head. "No, I don't think so."

I rear back in surprise and scoff. "You seriously aren't going to tell me your name?"

She shrugs and challenges me. "Why?"

"Why do I want to know your name?"

She nods and places a hand on her hip, jutting it out slightly as she does. "Yes, why? Are you planning on sending me flowers or are you just trying to get to know me better?"

She lifts her glass a little in the air. "Or do I owe you because you bought me a drink?"

A little unsure and a lot stunned by her response, I scratch my beard and frown down at her. "You're a spunky little thing, aren't you?"

She lifts her shoulders nonchalantly. "Maybe. Maybe I just know guys like you."

I raise my brows in surprise. "Guys like me?"

She nods and takes her hand off her hip to wave it up and down with a flourish around me. "Yes, guys like you: tall, dark and handsome."

She gives me another once over before continuing. "And I'd say rich based on your watch and shoes alone."

I give her my most dazzling smile. "You think I'm handsome?"

"See? That's all you heard." A small frown tugs her lips down. "Guys like you think they can throw their pretty little smiles around and we women are just supposed to fall at your feet."

"I wasn't expecting you to fall at my feet. I was just wondering what your name is."

She lifts the glass to her mouth, the ice clinking as she drains the rest of the vodka, and then takes a step closer to hand me the glass. "Like I said, thanks for the drink."

She looks me up and down one final time, shakes her head, muttering as she turns to leave, "Been there, done that. Not going there again."

As dumbfounded as I am, I can't help but chuckle under my breath. *Challenge accepted.*

I watch her walk back through the crowd, her beautiful bare back taunting me as she does. I raise my own glass in response, finishing the whiskey in one swallow, promising myself that this isn't over yet.

As I lower the glass, I notice Gage, my friend and photographer we hired for the evening, taking some pictures at the edge of the room. I quickly walk back to the bar, deposit the empty glasses, and ask Greta for two beers.

Grabbing them, I relocate Gage and make my way over to him.

"Hey, man! How's it going?" I hold one of the beers out to him, which he takes, a grateful look on his face.

"Thanks, man. I need this." He takes a long pull from the bottle. "The shoot is going great. I'm just about done I think. Just want to get some of your brother's speech and then I think I can wrap up."

"Thanks again for filling in last minute. I know Drew really appreciates it."

"No problem at all. It's easy work." He scowls and pulls at the collar of his shirt. "I just wish I didn't have to wear this damn thing. Hate having shit on my neck."

I can't help but chuckle, because I obviously know exactly how he's feeling, but I give him some crap anyway. "Toughen up and quit your bitching."

Gage points to my loosened collar and retorts. "Shut the fuck up! Where the hell is your tie?"

I grin broadly. "I don't work for my brother so I'll wear whatever the hell I want."

We laugh and take a couple more drinks in silence before Gage points his bottle toward the stage. "Looks like Drew might be getting ready to speak, so I'm going to go find a good spot."

"Okay, look me up after if you want to get another drink." I tip my bottle at him in goodbye and turn to see if I can find Hannah, Drew's wife. Scanning the crowd in front of the stage, I spot her and work my way over, a smile breaking across her face as she sees me, her hand lifting to wave me over.

I wave back and only miss half a beat in my step when I notice the woman in gold is standing next to Hannah, her features a mask of surprise as I approach and kiss Hannah on the cheek. "How's my favorite sister-in-law?"

She kisses me back and giggles. "I'm your only sister-in-law."

"Then you win, hands down."

I give her a wink and move to address the three people standing next to her, my eyes landing on my mystery woman, who is shaking her head, a small grin of defeat on her mouth. "Hi, I'm Benjamin Sapphire, Hannah's brother-in-law. I don't think we've met before."

"Oh, I'm sorry Ben." Hannah shifts quickly into hostess mode. "This is Drew's friend from college, Mika Kingsley, and his new bride, Raeva." She gives me a quick look of apology. "I thought you may have already known him."

"No worries at all, Hannah." I grasp Mika's firm grip in my own and shake it. "Nice to meet you both."

I give a warm smile to his wife and then move my attention to the woman on her right, extending my hand, unable to hide the devil in my grin. "And you are?"

She purses her lips and tilts her head, gracefully placing her hand in mine before finally bringing her eyes up to meet mine. "Jill Baldwin. Nice to meet you, Benjamin."

I 've got to hand it to the man; he's very resourceful. His lips curl up into a triumphant grin. *Damn it.* Of course, he had to be Benjamin freaking Sapphire.

"Jill Baldwin?" He repeats my name, as if he's mulling it over in his head. The timber of his voice traveling up my spine, awakening every nerve inside my body. Sex is literally seeping from his pores, and he is one thousand percent the type of guy I need to stay far, far away from. "I know I've heard that name before," he muses, still staring at me.

Dear God, it feels as if he looking right into my inner thoughts. I feel the heat rise in my cheeks. Nope. *Tall, dark, and off limits.* I remind myself sternly, forcing myself to get it together.

"I think you were supposed to be at the meeting I had with your brother last week," I reply sweetly. "But you had to cancel last minute?"

"Jill owns that amazing spa downtown." Hannah chimes in. "Serenity."

I met with Drew last week after Mika set up the meeting. He thought a partnership with Sapphire Resorts would be a great way for me to expand my business.

Quite frankly, in retrospect, I'm happy Ben wasn't at that meeting. I don't think I could have focused. Drew Sapphire is handsome, but his brother—oh my God—that man should be illegal. From his dark hair that's screaming to have my fingers running through it, to the intense gaze in his deep blue eyes, every inch of his impressive six feet is drawing me in like a moth to a flame. And that is a sure sign that I need to run for the hills, and fast.

"Well, I was sorry to miss the meeting that day, even

more so now," he replies smoothly as he flashes me a smile that could melt any pair of panties.

Good God, I need to get away from him. I force a tight smile. "Maybe next time. If you'll excuse me, I need to go powder my nose." I reach for Rae's arm. "Are you coming?" I ask her urgently.

Raeva raises a brow but nods. She kisses Mika on the cheek. "I'll be back in a bit, love," she tells him sweetly.

My heart is pounding against my chest as if it wants to escape. I take long strides toward the ladies' room, practically dragging poor Rae with me.

"Slow down, Jillybean. These are six-inch heels."

I slow my roll. "Sorry, Rae. I just had to get away," I explain as we step into the fancy bathroom. I look around. The Sapphires really take things to the next level.

Raeva chuckles. "I take it that Ben is tall, dark, and hell no?"

I groan. "I can't possibly do business with Benjamin Sapphire."

Raeva rolls her eyes at me. "Are you seriously going to walk away from a huge opportunity, just because you find a man attractive? I know I don't have to tell you how ridiculous that sounds."

I sigh. "Rae, guys like him—"

"Guys like him?"

"Yeah, too handsome, too rich, too..."

"Too what exactly? You do realize that you've just pretty much described my husband? And you adore him; I know you do." She admonishes.

"I adore him because he makes you happier than I've ever seen you."

Rae's face lights up like a Christmas tree. "That he does."

"Benjamin Sapphire is just not what I need in my life right now. I've been down that road plenty of times. I'm not…"

"Whoa, let me stop you right there. We are talking about a business deal, not marriage. If you don't want to date him, then don't. It's that simple."

As usual, my best friend makes total sense. "You're right, I'm being silly." *I am being ridiculous. No matter how gorgeous Ben is, I am in complete control of my emotions.* I tell myself in attempt to actually believe it.

"You good, Jillybean?"

"I'm good."

Raeva folds her arms around me and hugs me. After a beat, I pull away, holding her upper arms, and look at my beautiful friend. Her long, dark hair is cascading around her shoulders, and her full lips are painted the same red as the silky gown that seems to have been poured onto her. "Have I told you, you look amazing tonight?"

"Repeatedly, but thank you. And, might I add, right back at you. No wonder you had Ben drooling."

A girlish giggle escapes from my lips. "He was not drooling."

"Oh, please," Rae challenges.

We both are laughing as we walk out of the bathroom. "Is there any particular reason why you keep running off, Jill?"

I almost miss a step. I look up to find Benjamin Sapphire leaning against the wall across from the ladies' room.

"Well, that's my cue," Rae announces as she flashes me a wink.

"Traitor," I mouth at her. I watch her walk away for a moment, an enormous grin on her face, before I turn to face my accuser. "Going to the bathroom is running off?"

I'm surprised with how even my tone is. Judging from the look on Sapphire's face, it's thrown him off, too. But he recovers fast, a sexy grin lifting his lips as he approaches me.

"So, can I interest you in a drink at the bar then?"

"Look, um, Ben, is it?"

He closes the distance between us and cocks his head. "You know it is."

I bite my lower lip in an attempt to hide my smile; it's fun sparring with him. He's so close now, close enough for me to smell his cologne. Hints of clean soap and earthy scents tickle my nostrils, and it is taking everything I have to stop myself from inhaling deeply. Mercifully, I manage to collect myself.

Lifting my head, I look at him and smile sweetly. "I'm just not that into you."

His eyes sparkle brightly, a twinkle of amusement setting them ablaze. He takes another step closer, his right-hand slipping around my waist to pull me against him. It doesn't even occur to me to stop him.

Our gaze locks, and I feel his finger trail slowly from my shoulder to the very tip of my index finger. The gentle touch sets my body on fire. I gasp slightly, screaming inwardly to look away, but my irises are his willing prisoners. My body trembles against his, close enough now that I can feel how hard is chest is.

He leans in, agonizingly slow, and I know that I'm done for. His lips are mere inches from mine, his breath warm as it meets mine. My eyes flicker to his perfect mouth, and I swallow hard.

"Yes," he whispers against my lips. "I can see just *how little* you are into me." His lips gently brush my cheek as he releases me. The air is thick with desire, and I know it's not just mine. Ben shakes his head, a smirk on his face. "Stubborn little thing, aren't you?"

He takes my hand once more and lifts it to his lips. "I'll definitely be in touch."

And, with those parting words, he leaves me standing there in the hallway, somewhere between feeling bereft and dumbfounded.

"When's your next meeting with Jill Baldwin?" I burst into Drew's office and make myself comfortable in one of the wing back chairs in front of his desk. Glancing up, I'm met with a look of utter annoyance.

"Well, good morning to you, Benny." He waves his hand to the chair I'm already in. "Won't you come in and have a seat? It's not like I was working on anything." His brow arches high as he finishes, his voice laced with sarcasm. "Can I get you a cup of coffee perhaps?"

"You can get me Jill Baldwin's number," I retort, shaking off his edginess. *He's too wound up for his own good.*

"I'm sorry, whose number do you want?" His fingers are tapping in irritation on his desk.

"Jill Baldwin. Mika's wife's friend. Owns Serenity Spas. You had a meeting with her last week."

Realization dawns and a knowing smile dances on his

lips. "Ah, you must have met the lovely Ms. Baldwin at the opening, and now you're interested in a meeting. Am I correct?"

"Did you see her? She's absolutely stunning." I stand from the chair and begin pacing, trying to expend some of the restless energy coursing through my system. "But damn if she isn't playing hard to get."

"Yes, she's hard to miss. I can see why you're taken by her."

I stop and turn in his direction when I hear his fingers cease their movement. "But?" I know there's a but coming. Drew may be my younger brother, but there is no doubt that he's generally the more reasonable one of us.

"But," he gives me a hard stare, "I'm actually quite interested in having her incorporate her spas into our hotels and don't need you to interfere with that."

"So, let me help. If you think it's a good business decision, let me work to make the deal happen."

Drew chuckles and shakes his head. "I think we both know what kind of deal you're interested in when it comes to Ms. Baldwin. Go chase another skirt. This one is too important for you to mess with."

I move to stand in front of his desk and slap my palm down hard. "Damn it, this girl is different! I feel it in my bones."

My brother stands to his full height, which is two small inches taller than me, his blue eyes turning to steel. "Different because she said no? I'm sure that's a new concept for you, big brother."

"Fuck you, Drew." I move to stand next to him to show

I'm not intimidated by him in any way. "If memory serves correctly, I don't think it was too long ago that you found yourself in a very similar position. It was only chance that you ran into Hannah that day in the lobby that saved you."

I feel a little badly for shooting below the belt when I see Drew take a step back, his eyes widening in surprise, but the feeling goes away immediately when I hear his consent.

"Fine." He sits back in his seat and types something on his laptop. "I'll text you her information."

"No." Drew's eyes snap to mine in frustration. "I want you to set up another meeting with her, but I'll take the meeting, not you."

He stops typing and looks up at me, anger stewing close to the surface. "So, you're essentially going to trick her into a date with you?"

"No, it's a business meeting, but unfortunately, you aren't going to be able to make it, so I am generously going in your place to ensure discussions move forward." I flash him my cockiest grin and then continue. "Set it up for Thursday, 7:00 p.m. in the hotel restaurant at the new financial district location."

"A little late for a business meeting, don't you think?" His tone is wry and condescending at best.

"She won't say no to you. You're Drew 'Fucking' Sapphire." This time, I grace him with a genuine smile.

"You got that right." He finally cracks and lets a smirk escape before muttering, "You better not screw this deal up for us, Benny."

Three long nights later, I stroll into the Blue Ivy and address the hostess. "Good evening. I've got a table reserved under Sapphire."

"Of course, Mr. Sapphire." She takes two menus and leads me to a table. "I have you here, but if you'd prefer something else?"

"Yes, actually." I look toward one of the more private booths along the wall in the back of the room and move in that direction. "I'll take this. Can you show Ms. Baldwin to the table when she arrives, please?"

"Certainly." She sets the menus down and places the wine list in front of me. "Jeffrey will be over in just a moment. Do you need anything in the meantime?"

"No, thank you." I open the wine menu in dismissal and begin browsing the selections.

I'm fifteen minutes too early but couldn't stand sitting in my apartment any longer and also wanted the element of surprise when she arrived. I'm generally a whiskey or beer kind of guy, but given this is supposed to be a business meeting, wine seems like the wiser choice.

"Good evening, Mr. Sapphire, sir." A smartly dressed waiter in his mid-thirties stands before me, a white napkin folded neatly over his arm, a black pad at the ready. "I'm Jeffrey and will be your server for the evening. Would you care for something to drink from the bar, or perhaps a bottle of wine?"

"Jeffrey." I open the folder and point to the row of Pinot Noirs. "Let's try one of these bottles. Do you have a recommendation?"

"The 2014 Gaps Crown is very nice. It's from Oregon and has wonderful layers of floral and fruit flavors that aren't overly acidic."

"Great." I close the menu and smile up at him. "Let's do that then."

"Yes, sir." He walks quickly away to retrieve the wine, and I look at my watch for the twentieth time. Six-fifty. I wonder if she'll be prompt, but then consider what she must know is at stake if she goes into business with Sapphire Resorts and assume she will be.

Jeffrey is back before I can start another thought, twisting and turning the cork off with a soft pop and then handing it to me with a flourish. I smell it, pretending to know what I'm doing, and nod my head in approval. He pours a small taste into my glass, which I take, swish around, inhale, and taste.

My eyebrows fly up as the flavor of the wine bursts across my tongue and slides warmly down my throat. The wine is quite delicious, and I tell Jeffrey just that. He beams as if he had pressed the grapes himself and then pours more into my glass.

I raise my glass for another sip as he steps away, revealing a hidden Jill from his shadow, her lips pressed in a tight line, brows furrowed. Even with a grimace on her face, I cannot help but marvel again at how beautiful she is.

My eyes rake over her figure, hugged in a simple form-fitting dress of tan and black, made edgier by the cropped black leather jacket she's wearing. Her feet are also clad in black leather, but with three-inch heels, and she wears only simple diamond studs in her ears.

Standing, I greet her with my most charming smile, my hand extended. "Ms. Baldwin, you're so prompt."

She glares at my hand, ignoring it before responding tartly, "I thought I was meeting with the *other* Mr. Sapphire."

"Unfortunately, he had an unforeseen emergency and asked me to meet with you instead. He didn't want to cancel on such short notice or stall the discussions for the spas."

"Isn't that convenient?" One well-manicured brow arches sky high.

I chuckle lightly. "For me, perhaps." I move behind her and can't help but notice her eyes following, her neck craning as I place my hands on her shoulders. "Can I take your jacket?"

Seemingly resigned at being stuck with me, she shrugs as I slide the thin, soft material from her shoulders. Her arms are bare, and I notice, very tone, and wonder if she works out regularly or if it's great genetics. As I pull the jacket down her arms, I inhale her scent and immediately am reminded of coconuts and the sun.

She twirls around, seeming startled to realize she's only inches from me, and takes a sudden step back. "I don't know what game you're trying to play, Ben, but I can assure you right now that this is strictly a business dinner."

God, she's sexy when she's trying to be tough. I give her my most complacent smile and take her elbow, gently guiding her to the table and into the booth before sliding in next to her. "Of course. What else would it be?"

I lift the bottle that's been left by Jeffrey. "Wine?"

I really want to take him up on the offer. God knows I could use a drink. But seeing that I am already struggling to string together a coherent thought when I'm in his orbit, adding alcohol to the mix doesn't seem like a smart idea. *Crap, why does he have to be this ridiculously good looking?*

After taking a deep breath to calm my nerves, I immediately regret it. He's sitting right next to me, and the scent of him—clean mixed with woodsy and musky tones—is intoxicating.

I can't believe it's *him* that showed up. I regret my choice in clothing; it feels too constricted, too tight. I can literally feel his eyes roaming all over me, like a ghostly touch. I cross my legs and don't miss the fact that his eyes track the movement, his gaze hovering at my legs for a long moment before traveling back up to my face.

He looks at me expectantly, flashing his pearly whites. Everything about him is drawing me in, and I can't allow that. Alarm bells ring inside my head, instantly causing imaginary walls to shoot out of the ground and up to the ceiling.

"I'll stick with water, thank you," I tell him with an eerily calm voice, one that doesn't match what I am feeling at all.

"You don't like wine?"

"Quite the contrary; I love a good glass of wine. But, like

I said, this is a business dinner, and I don't mix business with pleasure."

"Ah, so, in your mind, you associate me with pleasure? I will take that as a win for me," he says with a smirk.

I scoff. "I associate you with a few things, Mr. Sapphire. Pleasure isn't on that list, I assure you. I am here to discuss business. If that isn't the case, then I will get up and leave right now."

When I move to do just that, he gently places a hand on my arm. "Listen, I'm sorry," he says sheepishly. "I think we got off on the wrong foot. Can we start over? Please?"

He actually looks contrite and sounds sincere, and I can't help but feel a little bad. I sigh. "Okay, let's start over," I concede.

He visibly relaxes, his shoulders dropping on an exhale, and I tense up more in response. "Ms. Baldwin, thank you for joining me tonight. I know you were expecting my brother, but I assure you that I am just as invested in the company as he is."

I realize it is entirely possible that I am putting too much stock in my belief that this is a set-up. After all, he is a Sapphire and this deal could be lucrative for all parties involved. To think that he would orchestrate this meeting just to get into my pants seems a little arrogant. I mean, I know I'm an attractive woman, but that man is sex on legs and certainly doesn't need to beg. Why would he go through all this if it wasn't for business?

I smile at him. "I've been looking forward to the meeting, Mr. Sapphire. I—"

"Please, call me Ben." He interrupts with a shake of his

head. "Mr. Sapphire is my father; I have no desire to be called that."

"Okay… Ben." Just saying his name causes a tingling feeling in my belly. "And you can call me Jill, if you'd like."

"Perfect." He flashes a quick smile. "Thank you, Jill."

I nod my head and continue. "As I was saying, I have been looking forward to this meeting because I think a collaboration between your resorts and my spa would be a happy marriage."

Ben smiles, and I fight the urge to touch the dimple that appears. He hands me a menu, and I pretend to read it. Instead, I am inwardly trying to collect myself. My heart rate is accelerated, every single nerve ending in my body is at high attention, and my stomach is tied up in a thousand knots. *Why the hell does he make me so damn nervous?*

The server approaches the table and asks if we are ready to order. My eyes dart over to Ben, who is studying my expression. I force a smile and nod. I order the first thing I see and hand the waiter the menu. Ben orders his food, and the server pours us both some water before leaving us to our discussion.

"My brother tells me that one of the reasons he was so keen to meet you in the first place is the development of your own product line and special services. I understand it's quite revolutionary. Can you tell me more?"

"Of course." I pull my catalog from my attaché, place it on the table, and slide it toward him. I'm impressed he's actually done his homework. He opens it as I tell him about my skincare line, the painless hair removal, and about the special rejuvenating facials we offer. Much to my surprise, he actually hangs on my every word. He seems genuinely interested, asking me follow-up questions and taking notes. Now that I am talking about my passion, I feel relaxed and in control.

The food arrives, so I place the catalog back in my attaché while Ben stows his notebook away. Our dinners are placed in front of us, and I'm relieved to see I ordered a salad. The server pours more wine for Ben and asks me if I would like a glass, too.

"Actually, I'd love a glass," I say with a smile. I expect Ben to comment, but he simply smiles and cuts his steak. I accept the glass from our server and take a sip of the blood red liquid, nearly moaning at the taste. It's delicious. I tell him so and he beams at me.

"This is one of my very favorite wines," Ben confesses as the server strides off.

A chuckle escapes my lips.

"That's funny?"

"No, it's just that you don't really strike me as a wine guy."

"That is an astute observation. What, pray tell, would you say is my poison of choice?"

This is too easy. "Hmmm, that is a hard question." I purse my lips as I pretend to mull it over. "You definitely strike me as a bourbon kinda guy."

Ben raises a brow and a small smile tugs at my lips. "Is that right? What brings you to that conclusion?"

"I could lie and tell you that I guessed, but I won't. I remember what drink you ordered the night we met." I grin with a little wink.

"You remember what drink I ordered?" His brows arch in feigned delight. "Well, Jill, if I didn't know any better, I would swear that I made an impression on you."

He has no idea. "I'm glad you know better."

His lips curl up into a smile, revealing those dimples of his. I drain my glass and warmth spreads through my belly, knowing it isn't the wine causing this stir inside of me.

"Would you like some more wine?" he asks as he hovers the bottle above my glass.

I am inclined to say yes, because part of me wants to prolong the evening. But a nagging voice in the back of my head is telling me to go. I am not setting myself up for disappointment and heartbreak. I need to get off this road. "I think I have had enough. Thank you, Ben," I state politely.

He nods and places the bottle back on the table.

"In fact, I think I should probably call it a night. If you have any more questions, you can email me."

"You're right, it is getting late." Ben motions the server and requests the check, handing him his credit card without even looking to find out how much the dinner costs.

Our server returns swiftly, and Ben puts his credit card back into his wallet. He hesitates for a moment, but then slides out of the booth and picks up my coat. I follow suit and smoothly glide out of the booth. An involuntarily shiver courses through my body as he helps me into it.

"Let me walk you out," he offers. "I'll help you catch a cab."

"Actually, I have a driver waiting for me, but thank you."

"Let me walk you to your car then."

"All right."

We walk through the restaurant, which for the time of night is still very crowded. Ben places his hand on the small of my back, and my breath catches. I notice some longing looks being thrown his way, and I hate to admit that I loathe them. A chilly New York breeze greets us as we step outside onto the teeming sidewalk.

"Well, I think this was a very successful *business* dinner," he tells me as we walk toward my waiting car.

"I think so, too. I am very excited." Upon our approach, the driver gets out of the car and moves to open the door for me, but Ben beats him to it. I get into the back seat and look up at him. "I look forward to further discussions."

He presses the button on the window, lowering it before shutting the door. He holds out his hand, and I place mine in it. He brings it to his lips and presses a small, sweet kiss on the back of my hand before letting it go. "Goodnight, Jill."

"Goodnight, Ben," I croak.

Our eyes lock, and even as the driver starts to pull into traffic, I don't look away. He smiles at me, and I give him a small wave. I don't take my eyes off him until we turn the corner.

I'm so screwed.

CHAPTER
Three

I walk into the lobby, nod a greeting to the doorman, and stride toward the elevator. "I'm expected."

"Very good, sir." He moves to the phone to alert my presence. "I'll just let them know you're on the way up."

I step into the elevator, press the PH button, and stare at the wall during the thirty second ride until the doors swish open. I walk into the hallway, approach their door, and raise my hand to knock, but it's pulled open before I can connect.

"Benjamin!" A beaming Hannah stands in front of me, Brody seated firmly on her hip, his head leaning on her shoulder, thumb in his mouth. "What brings you over in the middle of the day?" She steps out of the way and motions for me to come inside. "Not that I'm complaining! You know I love seeing you."

I reach for Brody. "Here, let me take him. You look like your arm is going to fall off."

Sighing gratefully, she shifts him from her arms to mine.

"He's been a handful these last few weeks. He won't let me put him down."

I adjust him so that he's resting with his head down on my shoulder and kiss the top of his downy locks, inhaling and appreciating his baby smell. *Why do they always smell so damn good?*

He looks like a mini Drew; same dark hair and striking blue eyes. "No Gracie?" I think my favorite part of visiting Hannah is getting to see what kind of witty quips her six-year-old daughter will throw my way.

"School." She turns and starts toward the kitchen. "Come on, you want some coffee?"

"Sure, that sounds great." I follow her, stepping over toys along the way, and sit on a stool while she moves around prepping the coffee for us.

"You hungry?" She walks to the fridge and pulls the door open. "I can make you a sandwich or a salad if you want?"

"Just coffee is great." I smile at her and think how lucky my brother is to have someone this loving in his life. Although their beginning was definitely a little unconventional, nothing about their life today is.

They share a love and devotion for each other that I can't help but admire and hope to find myself one day. I'm thirty-six years old, almost thirty-seven. I'm getting tired of the chase, nameless girls, and my empty apartment.

"So, you going to tell me what's on your mind?" She lifts a brow as she sets a big mug in front of me, steam rising from the hot, black liquid.

I take a sip and grin. "What, you think I have a motive? Just couldn't stop by to see my favorite sister?"

"I see you almost every day, Ben." She comes up beside me and pulls a now sleeping Brody out of my arms, and I watch as she places him gently in a nearby pack-n-play before walking back to sit on the stool beside mine. "That's how I know you've got something on your mind."

I smile sheepishly into my coffee before looking back up at her. "Guilty as charged I guess."

"All right, spill then." She pulls her cup of coffee closer and takes a sip.

"There's a girl." Before I can get another word out, she starts laughing. My brow scrunches up in confusion at her response.

She slaps her hand over her mouth and shakes her head as she gets her laughing under control. "It's Jill Baldwin, isn't it?"

My eyes open wide, and she smacks her hand on the counter when she registers my surprised look.

"Uh-huh! I knew it! I saw the way you looked at her at the opening celebration!" She hits her hand on my leg this time and smiles wide. "And Drew may have mentioned you have a little crush on her."

"Fucking, Drew." I mutter, then sheepishly nod. "But yeah, it's Jill Baldwin."

"I knew it!" She claps her hands in delight and beams like she just won the lottery. Women are strange. "Okay, what can I do to help?"

"She's playing hard to get, and let's face it, Hannah, you wrote the book on that one."

Her mouth falls open as her brows shoot up. "Benjamin

Sapphire, I did not play hard to get. My situation was completely different and you know it."

"Okay, if you say so." I raise a brow in doubt. "The point is, she says everything is about business and insists on keeping things that way, but there is a chemistry there. When we're together, talking, just being in the same space, it's different than anything else I've ever felt before, and I know she feels it, too. But, damn it, she's fighting it tooth and nail."

"Are you sure it's not just the fact that she's saying no?" She raises her hand to stop me from arguing. "Don't get mad at the question; it's a fair one. I mean, let's face it, Ben, you don't hear that word very often."

I roll my eyes. "I hear it more than you think, and no, that's not the issue. Because you're right; for every one person that says no, there are ten that say yes."

"Well, aren't you just special, little lover boy?" She's joking when she says it, but what she doesn't realize is that it's not a title I want.

I can't remember the last time I spent an actual night with anyone and felt happy about it the next morning, or had a conversation with a woman that intrigued me. Most of the time, women approach and proposition me, not the other way around. And spending every night by yourself gets lonely. It fills a void but definitely not anything in my heart.

I think she realizes she's hit a nerve because she reaches over and grabs my hand. "I'm sorry, Ben. I was only joking. You are one of the most caring men I've ever met in my life.

Let's not forget that I know this better than just about anyone."

She's referring to her first husband, Jackson, who was killed in action shortly after I lost my leg. Losing him and two other brothers-in-arms was almost more than I could bear, especially while I was dealing with the loss of half my leg. With help, though, I did get through the losses and started a gym for disabled veterans. It's free and there for anyone that needs its services. It's named after her late-husband.

I squeeze her hand and force a smile. "I know."

"So, we need to figure out how to get Jill to take you seriously." She taps her finger on her chin, thinking, and then suddenly sits up straight and points her finger in the air. "I know what you need to do!"

"Okay, let's hear it." I can't wait to see what she's come up with.

"Well, you are definitely interested in her business, right? And, that seems to be the most important thing to her at the moment, right?"

"Definitely a top priority for her. And, yes, me too. It would actually be a great partnership." I waggle my brows. "In every way if I can help it."

She rolls her eyes. "Oh, Benny."

I frown at her use of Drew's nickname for me. "Keep going."

"Then you need to go check out her business. You can use it as an in to see her again. Go to her spa, say you want to see and experience the services in person. You need her to first believe that you're committed to the business partnership before she's ever going to take a chance on you personally."

"That's it?" It seems to simple.

"Yes, that's it." She reaches for her phone, brings up a number, and then puts the phone to her ear after pressing call.

"Hey, Jill! It's Hannah Sapphire. How are you?" She's silent for a minute, nodding her head as she listens to Jill. "Yes, I had a great time at the opening, as well. I was so glad you were able to come. I was actually wondering if you could help me out with something?"

She gets up, pacing back and forth in the kitchen as she talks. "Drew and his brother Ben have worked so hard getting the resort up and running, and I was hoping to treat them to some services at your spa. They need to relax for a bit!"

She's nodding her head again. "Yes, you are so right! It's a wonderful way for them to see first-hand what you do!"

She nods her head a few more times and then gives me a big thumbs-up. "Yes, I can get them there on Thursday for you. Not a problem at all. Thank you so much. Let's get together ourselves soon, too! You, me, and Raeva for lunch! Okay, bye, Jill!"

Ending the call, she looks up at me with a victory grin on her face. "Step one of Operation Get Jill is complete! You and Ben have a full spa package scheduled for this Thursday at noon!"

I smile brightly back at her and wrap her in a hug. "You are the best! Thanks!"

Two days later, Drew and I walk into Serenity ten minutes before noon for our appointment. "This was a good idea, brother. The best way for us to determine just how top of the line their products and services are."

"You have your wife to thank for this, not me. She came up with the brilliant idea."

"Ah, yes, the 'Operation Get Jill' plan. Hannah did mention that." He shakes his head while giving me a hard eye roll. "I'm trying to forget about that part of this visit."

I grin over at him. "But that's the best part of the whole afternoon." Our conversation pauses as we're greeted at reception and then shown to a locker room where we can change. I thought Jill was going to meet us, so I voice my disappointment to Drew when I don't see her.

"I'm sure she's quite busy. Perhaps she got pulled into something else. Besides, we're here for several hours. I'm sure we'll see her at some point."

We're led to a medium sized room where two massage tables are set up. Two women are waiting in the room and smile when we enter, one of them speaking. "Good afternoon, gentlemen. Jill booked this room for you, in case you wanted to discuss business during your massage, but if you'd prefer a single room, we can accommodate that for you as well."

I look at Drew, and we both shrug in unison. "This is fine."

"Wonderful. We'll step out and let you get situated on the table. Just slide under the sheet, and we'll start face down."

The women leave and we both move to a table. I sit on the table, bend down and pull my prosthetic off below the knee, then lean it against the table. Drew's already sliding under the sheet as I stand and balance on one leg to take my robe off and then slide under my own. The room is warm, and soft melodic music is playing over speakers hidden somewhere. It's relaxing, and I chalk up one point for Jill and her business.

"So, do you really like her, or is it just the thrill of the chase?" Drew asks from his side of the room, his words slightly mumbled as his face is lying sideways on the table.

"It's not the chase." I scoff. "Well, you know, a little chase is always fun, but that's not it. Yes, she absolutely may be one of the most beautiful woman I've laid eyes on, but it's more than that. There's a spark there. She's challenging and smart and isn't afraid or intimidated by me one little bit. It's refreshing to find a woman who is utterly sure of herself and knows what she wants but also shows some vulnerability."

The door clicks open, and I hear two sets of feet shuffle quietly in. "Any objection to oils?" one of the women asks. Drew and I both grunt out a, "No."

I feel the sheet being adjusted and then a slight gasp as all movement stills for a minute. I'm never sure if it's because of the tattoos covering my back or if it's my leg, but the pause is so short, and I'm so used to it by now, that I dismiss it as quickly as it occurred.

"So, are you going to ask her on a real date?" Drew mumbles between a moan.

I feel oil on my back and then let out a long sigh when hands start to work my shoulders. I boxed for two hours yesterday, and I'm sore as hell today.

"That's the plan." I groan as the fingers dig hard into a knot on my back. "But, first, I think I have to get her to admit she likes me."

Jill 15 minutes earlier...

I could have killed Anna a few minutes ago. Rationally, I know it isn't her fault that the daycare called to inform her that Casey—her little girl—has a fever, and thus per policy, needs to be collected from daycare. I know she had no intention of leaving me high and dry. But still, I can't help but feel annoyed that she put me in this situation, today of all days.

The spa is completely booked, and I have no other available staff. Seeing as today is all about impressing the Sapphire men, I have no other choice but to step in myself. We walk back into the room after a few minutes have passed by. Aisha asks if they object to oils, and neither does. She has already positioned herself beside Drew to start his massage and I chastise myself for my predicament. *I should have insisted before that she take Ben.*

I gently pull back the sheet, a small gasp escaping from

my lips as I absorb the sight before me. Never in my life have I ever seen someone's back and thought it was sexy.

This man's back is a work of art—all muscle and sun-kissed skin decorated with ink. I knew he had tattoos but would have never imagined that so many graced his skin. At first glance, I think it's just a tribal tattoo, but upon further inspection, I find several animals sketched into his back. The large wolf particularly grabs my attention, and I long to trace my fingers over the fur that looks so real.

Grabbing a few bottles from the warmer, I mix the different oils together in my hands. I smooth the oil all over his broad shoulders and his back, tracing each muscle. I've never really been a tattoo kinda girl, but his are beautiful, not to mention the canvas.

I am so enthralled that I nearly miss when Drew mumbles something about asking "her" out on a real date. My heart rate accelerates and begins to knock against my ribcage as my fingers kneed his firm flesh. *Is he talking about me?*

"That's the plan," he says as my fingers make short work of a knot in his back. He groans, and the sound of it causes a stir in my belly. He tells Drew that he has to get "her" to admit she likes him. And, I know then, without a shadow of a doubt, that he is talking about me.

Frankly, it annoys me, and not just because he is cocky enough to think that I might have more feelings for him than I am admitting to. Mostly, it's because I know that his pretentious self is right, even though I don't want him to be.

Drew chuckles. "How are you planning to pull that off,

Romeo? It's not like your charms have worked on her so far."

I bite my bottom lip to stifle my laugh. I'm beginning to like Drew more and more.

"What do you know?" Ben grumbles. He sounds sullen, and it is adorable. My hands continue to explore, and I have a hard time keeping my inner dialog under control. As my fingers sweep across his back and dip lower to his buttocks, I nearly groan myself. It's rare for a man to have a nice backside, but Ben? Yeah, the man wrote the book on having a great ass. I tell myself to focus. You'd think I've never done this before.

I pull the sheet back up to his shoulders and position myself at the bottom of the table. I'm about to lift the sheet when I notice a prosthetic leg leaning against the table. I tilt my head, glancing at the table beside me, but neither Drew nor Aisha is paying attention to me. I lift the sheet to position it so his lower half is exposed and see that it's indeed Ben's prosthetic. I had no idea that he had lost part of his leg.

Shaking my head, I attempt to clear my thoughts, becoming even more curious about the man beneath me. I rub some more oil onto my hands and start to massage his upper legs. He stiffens for a short moment when I slide my hands near his stump but soon relaxes under my fingers.

Maybe, I have been judging him unfairly? Maybe, my opinion of him has more to do with my own fears? Maybe, I should just give the man a chance? Maybe, I have been trying so hard to keep him at arm's length, to deny—even to myself—that there is an obvious attraction between us. But, honestly, I am not sure I can muster up the will to deny it anymore.

"You know what?" Ben says.

"What?" Drew mumbles.

"I'm just gonna ask her." He declares.

Drew lifts his head toward Ben and opens his eyes. His expression is one of complete surprise when his gaze lands on me, a smirk slowly appearing on his face. A small smile tugs at my mouth in response as I shrug.

"You are just going to ask her what, Benny?" Drew continues to look at me as he continues his conversation with his brother.

I smile back at Drew and shake my head.

"I'm just going to lay it on the table."

"You are laying on a table."

"You know what I mean, asshole," he says, clearly a little irritated. "If I go to her and just tell her how I feel, ask for a chance to get to know her better over dinner or something, what else can she say besides yes?"

My brow shoots up, and Drew cocks his head, scratching his chin as he attempts to mask his growing smile. I pull the sheet back to cover Ben, then make my way toward the head of the table.

I lean in close until my mouth is right by his ear. "I'll tell you what else she can say."

I grin wickedly when his head shoots off the table to lock eyes with mine. "I'm not your typical kinda girl. I expect gentleman-like behavior—opened doors, pull out my chair type of thing. If you are running late, pick up a phone and call or don't bother showing up. If you can live with that, you can pick me up tomorrow night at seven."

I stand straight and walk toward the door, just as Ben pushes himself up off the table. I reach for the handle but pause briefly. "Oh, and Ben, any man that wants to take me out to dinner has to bring me flowers. White lilies are my favorites, if you care."

Ben stares back at me, shock apparent on his face for only a second before he flashes me a stunning smile. "White lilies, huh?"

I smile and nod.

"Duly noted."

I close the door behind me and scurry to my office to catch my breath, or at least until my heartbeat slows down. I need a minute or two just to collect my thoughts. The Sapphire men are scheduled to be here for most of the afternoon, but luckily for me, I can hide in here while my staff takes over.

I try to focus on work for a while, but thoughts of Ben, his very naked body, and a date with him tomorrow keep distracting me. I need some girl time to help me collect my thoughts. I pull my phone out and go to the group text between myself, Rae, and Mik and tell them that I need an emergency cocktail meeting tonight. I press send, my fingers drumming on my desk as I wait for their responses, a knock on my door distracting me.

"Yes?" I call out to my closed door.

The door opens, and Sage, the front desk girl, sticks her head in. "Hey Jill?"

"Yes?"

"There is a delivery for you."

"Okay. Do I need to sign for it or something?"

"Um, no, but I think you might want to come and see this."

I rise and walk toward the door but step back when it opens wider and several delivery people enter, and begin filling up my office with white lilies. A girlish giggle escapes my lips as my cheeks heat up and flush a light pink. The last person to walk in is holding a bouquet so large that I don't notice it's Ben until he places the flowers on top of my desk.

"I see that you don't half-ass things," I say with a small chuckle.

He smirks and waves a hand across my flower-filled room. "Go big or go home."

"That is a dangerous precedent you are setting for yourself, Mr. Sapphire," A playful tone to my response.

"I'm okay with that," I inhale his scent as he leans closer. "I think you're worth it."

I'm smiling so big, my face hurts. I've got to hand it to the man. He is good.

"I'd like to properly ask you out." He looks at me, brow raised, an expectant look on his handsome face.

"By all means," I retort, happy to play this game.

He flashes me those dimples of his, and I know I am a goner. "Jill, I'd love to take you out for dinner tomorrow night if you are free?"

"It's kind of last minute. I will have to check my schedule," I deadpan, glancing around the large bouquet of flowers to feign a look at my calendar.

"Of course," he says, one side of his mouth quirking up.

"Hmmm," I tell him. "I think I might be able to squeeze you in."

We both smirk at one another, and he takes a step forward.

"Does seven work for you?" he asks.

"It does." I walk to my desk, jot my address and cell number down on my business card, and then stroll back to hand it to him.

Ben leans in to place a gentle kiss on my cheek as he slides the card from my fingers. I close my eyes and let out a sigh as his lips make contact against my skin. "See you tomorrow night, Jill."

"Looking forward to it, Ben."

Did I mention how screwed I was?

The town car pulls up in front of her building precisely five minutes before seven, and I realize I'm nervous. I can't remember the last time I felt like this; well, at least, about picking a woman up for a date. There were plenty of times overseas that I was more than nervous, but those were life and death situations. This is definitely not that. I take a deep breath and tell the driver I'll be just a minute.

I step out of the car and approach her building but stop in my tracks, my heart skipping two beats in my chest as I see her exit the building. Did I just say this isn't a life or death situation? Because what she's wearing literally knocks the wind out of me. She sashays up to me, hips swaying lightly back and forth as her heels click on the pavement, her smile brightening the dusky night sky.

I sweep my gaze up her body, clad in a little black dress, but not your typical LBD. Oh, no, not my Jill. This one hugs every curve of her body, starting with the high neckline that is followed by two, black sheer strips; the second strip revealing just a peek of her cleavage. The dress falls a few inches above her knees, but there's a slit in one side of the skirt that exposes almost her entire thigh with each step.

She's teasing me, and the smile she's giving me says she knows it. She comes to a stop in front of me, and I reach out to gently clasp her hand in mine, raise it to my lips, and brush a soft kiss against her knuckles. "You look exquisite."

Her cheeks flush just the lightest color of pink as she casts her eyes down to my feet and then leisurely up my body until she meets my gaze. "You look pretty fine yourself, Mr. Sapphire."

I grimace at being called Mr. Anything but don't want to start the evening off on the wrong foot, so I smile and nod my head in thanks. "I would have come up."

"I was ready. No need." She fidgets with her small clutch and smiles. "Am I dressed appropriately? You didn't say where we were going?"

"You're perfect." I move my hand to her elbow and guide her to the town car where the driver is already waiting with an open door. I help her in and then move around to the other side of the car, settling myself in beside her.

As soon as I sit in the enclosed space with her, I'm assaulted by her scent and close my eyes for a minute to try to identify it's origin. It's unique and not the overly sweet perfume other women often wear. This is light and fresh and reminds me of how the air smells in the forest after a summer storm.

"Are you okay?" Her voice is a bit timid.

My eyes fly open, and I turn my head so I can meet her gaze. "I was smelling you."

"Smelling me?" Her brows furrow in confusion.

"Yes." I lean my head forward so that my nose is almost touching her neck, and I inhale deeply. I lift my gaze back to her, not pulling away. "You smell like the rain, clean and crisp and pure."

Her hand moves to her neck as she pulls back from me just a bit, and I realize I might be invading her space a little too soon, so I pull myself back up straight. "Sorry. I didn't mean to make you uncomfortable."

She drops her hand down onto mine as she provides me with a warm smile. "You aren't making me uncomfortable. It's a nice compliment. Thank you."

I turn my palm so I can lace her fingers in mine, pulling it into my lap, my thumb sweeping back and forth across hers. Her skin is soft and warm against mine. "You're welcome."

"So, are you going to tell me where we're going?" She tilts her head to one side as she asks.

"You don't like surprises?" I raise an eyebrow in response.

"Only good surprises."

"This is a good one. I promise."

She chuckles. "Already making promises?"

I frown. "Is that a bad thing?"

"Only when you don't deliver, and in my experience, I've learned most men don't."

Immediately feeling challenged by her statement, I raise my brows. I grasp her hand a little tighter and yank her flush to me, a yelp of surprise escaping her painted red lips which are now a breath away from mine. I take her face gently in my other hand and meet her hard stare.

"Let me assure you, Jill, I'll deliver on any promise I make to you. And I also guarantee you won't be disappointed because I'm not like most men, and I don't like being compared to them." I cock my head closer. "Understand?"

My voice is just short of a growl, but she doesn't look scared. She looks aroused. Her breath is falling in short little pants, and her gaze keeps moving from my eyes to my mouth, her pink tongue darting out to run across her lips as she nods. "Got it."

I move my hand slightly and run my thumb over the same trail her tongue just took, her breath inhaling sharply as I do, her eyes fluttering shut. I lean in, but instead of kissing her and doing the expected, I trail my nose across her cheek, down her neck, and then up to her ear, brushing against her soft locks and finally whispering, "I could kiss you right now. I want to. So badly. But in *my* experience, *really* good things are worth the wait."

She pulls back sharply from my grasp and purses her lips, fire burning in her eyes. "You, Benjamin Sapphire, are a tease."

I give her my most devilish grin. "And you, Jill Baldwin, are fun to tease." Her mouth falls open to respond, but I point out the window and speak. "We've arrived, and just in the nick of time, I think."

"Just in the nick of time for you, I think," she retorts.

I step out of the car and motion for the driver to stay as I move to the other side to open Jill's door. "Is there a restaurant in this marina?" I watch as she swivels her head back and forth in search of one.

"Sort of." I take her hand and start toward one of the docks where a large yacht is moored. "Come on, it's this way."

"Are we going on that?" She points to the boat, eyes wide.

I'm thrilled to have surprised her and maybe even a little proud that I can share such a luxurious experience with her. The yacht is actually my parents, but they rarely use it these days. They were more than happy to lend it to me, as well as the staff, for the evening. Especially after they found out that I'd be taking a date on board. I think, they're afraid I'm never going to settle down. "We sure are. Do you like boats?"

"Um, sure. I mean, this is more than a boat. But are you sure I'm really dressed for this?" She pulls back on my hand, stalling our forward progress.

I chuckle at her dress concerns. "Jill, this is a luxury yacht. You won't have to do any mooring or sailing on this. You're absolutely perfect."

"So, we're actually going to leave the dock and go out on the water?" Her voice rises an octave.

"Yep." I start moving forward again. "The staff have a wonderful dinner they're preparing for us, and we can relax and watch the stars as we eat and take in the New York City skyline."

"That sounds wonderful." She stammers as we reach the vessel. "I've never been on a luxury yacht before."

I help her onto the yacht and lead her to the main salon where the staff are waiting. Introductions are made before the captain excuses himself to get our trip underway. Heather, one of the attendants, pours us each a glass of champagne, and I usher Jill toward the deck.

"Isn't it beautiful?" I want to make sure she's comfortable, but I also am doing my damndest to try to impress this woman.

"It really is gorgeous. It feels so decadent." She wraps her arms around herself and shivers as we approach the railing. I shrug my jacket off and drop it over her shoulders as I move to stand behind her and shield the wind.

"Is it too cold for you? We can go back inside." I run my hands lightly up and down her arms to warm her.

"No, it's fine. I like the fresh air." She turns her head and gives me a smile. "Thank you for your jacket."

"Let me know if you get too cold. I can get you a blanket." I step closer to her so the heat of my body insulates her. She leans back against me and lets out a long sigh, which in turn makes my heart race. I want her to feel relaxed with me, comfortable. I want this to be one of the best nights of her life and feel like we're off to a perfect start.

"**I**s it too cold for you? We can go back inside," Ben asks with concern in his voice as he gently rubs my arms on either side, trying to warm me.

Oh, God, please no, not inside.

He's very sweet, and I hate that this date is probably going to be ruined by my seasickness. I am inwardly kicking myself, knowing I should have spoken up when I had the chance. Now, I have to put on my big girl panties and power through. He steps closer, pressing his body against mine.

I am a little taken aback by how natural this feels, but I don't dwell, and let myself enjoy the moment. I lean back against him, and a soft contented sigh falls from my lips. With my head resting against his chest, I listen to his heart beating. It's accelerated, like mine. Ben leans in and kisses the top of my head. I lift my gaze, and his eyes fix on mine. We stare at each other for a moment. Suddenly, he spins me around and pushes my back against the railing, caging me with one arm and cupping my face with the other.

"Fuck waiting," he snarls.

His lips press against mine, gentle little pecks at first but it's not enough. I throw my arms around his neck, the jacket slipping from my shoulders, my body no longer chilly. I deepen the kiss, and while it starts off sweetly, our tongues dancing around each other, exploring, tasting each other, it soon turns more frantic, almost desperate.

Any feeling of nausea or cold is forgotten as this man expertly invades my mouth. My entire body feels like it is on fire, and the heat between my thighs is almost unbearable. There is no denying that I want him. *Right now.* Unfortunately, we are interrupted by the clearing of a throat and both turn to face a very red-faced staff member, whose name currently escapes me.

"I am so sorry, Mr. Sapphire. I wanted to let you know that dinner is being served."

Ben recovers much faster than I do, because he flashes her a smile and thanks her. He holds out his hand, and I take it without a shred of hesitation. I'll follow him anywhere right now.

We head inside, and I inhale a sharp breath as I appraise the sight before me. The table is beautifully set, and the food smells delicious. I can't disguise the smile beaming from my face when I notice the vase of white lilies on the center of the table.

Ben pulls out my chair and I lower myself in to it. He makes his way across from me and gracefully drops into his seat, flashing that grin that makes me weak in the knees. The girl that caught us making out on the deck walks in with plates of appetizers, and I feel my cheeks heating when her gaze meets mine. She smiles at me sweetly and gives me a wink, putting me at ease.

"This is stunning."

"Thank you," he replies, eyes fixed on me. "You're stunning."

My cheeks heat under his scrutiny, lifting at his compliment. I place my napkin on my lap, and I begin moving some of the starters to my plate. The boat begins to sway, the rocking motion seeming to intensify with each bite I take.

I set my fork down and blow out a long breath, hoping to settle the roiling motion that's begun in my belly. Ben's brow furrows, concern evident on his face as he peers over the food at me.

"Are you okay?" He points to the pitcher of water on the table. "Would you like some water?"

I can feel my stomach contents coming up, and my eyes widen and flash over to meet his. Panicked, I scan the room, trying to search for a bathroom. I can't see myself, but I'm convinced that I must be a lovely shade of green at this moment.

"Bathroom," I gasp.

Ben jumps out of his chair and is over to me in a heartbeat. He lifts me into his arms and carries me swiftly to the bathroom. I drop to my knees in front of the toilet and am mortified as my insides gush out like a tsunami. Ben kneels beside me and holds my hair with one hand while stroking my back with the other.

When it finally feels as if the sickness is letting up, embarrassment rears its ugly head. I cover my mouth with my hand and stand, stumbling toward the sink. I turn on the faucet and rinse out my mouth, I look up and grimace when I see my reflection in the mirror.

"Are you okay?" he asks me. "Is it motion sickness?"

I bite my lip as our eyes meet in the mirror and I nod.

"Shit." He rakes a hand over his beard. "Has this happened before? I would have never taken the yacht out if I had known you were prone to sea sickness."

"It may have happened once or twice before." I reply sheepishly. I close the lid on the toilet and slump down onto the seat, my stomach still not feeling its best. "You went to so much trouble to set this beautiful dinner up. I didn't want to ruin it and hoped—well prayed, if I'm being honest — that the seas would be calm enough that I'd be okay." I force a weak smile. "So much for that theory."

"You could have told me. Dinner would have been just as nice moored to the dock." Ben kneels down in front of me, taking my hands into his. "You don't have to hide things from me. I'm not a fragile flower that will fall apart if plans have to change."

He rises to his full height, pulling me up with him. "Let's get this baby turned around and get you feeling better, yeah?"

"Please." I practically plead, my hand flat on my turbulent tummy.

He smiles and asks me if I will be okay for a moment, and I tell him I'll be fine. He comes back only a short moment later and wraps a blanket around me before he leads me back onto the deck. We sit in complete silence with his arm draped around me.

I am grateful when we make it back to the dock so quickly. We thank the staff, and Ben wastes no time ushering me off the boat and onto the dock. My legs are still a little wobbly, and he must notice, because he wraps an arm around me, pulling me up against his frame to steady me.

We make it to the car, and he helps me inside, closing the door once I'm settled, then moving around the other side to climb in beside me. His eyes, as dark as the night, analyze me. "Feeling better?"

I nod, my pride swallowing away any words I might have.

"I guess we're going to have to try this again." He flashes me a glimpse of his cocky grin as he continues. "But on land this time."

I look at the man that just held my hair as I lost every last bit of what was in my stomach, and am overcome with an unfamiliar feeling. Not able to put any words together at this moment in time, I just nod.

Screwed? I'm fucked.

Frustration reigns supreme as I walk around the car to climb in beside Jill. Have I made her feel so uncomfortable that she couldn't share the truth with me about her aversion to being on the water?

Reasonably, I know she was only trying to make the best out of what ended up being a bad predicament for her, but I want her to feel she can be completely open with me and know I won't be upset. I think it's the soldier in me. I'm used to my team letting me know any weaknesses so we can protect and keep each other's backs safe. And damn it if I don't feel like I need to protect Jill.

I open the door and lower myself into the seat next to her. One look in her direction has me doing a complete one-eighty. She's practically curled herself up like a kitten, the blanket from the yacht wrapped around her, making her tiny form somehow look even smaller. Her eyes are down-cast, her skin still so pale from the turbulence her body felt on the boat. She musters a small smile and peeks up at me from under her dark lashes.

"Feeling better?" It's hard to tell quite honestly, especially when she only answers with a nod.

"I guess we're going to have to try this again?" I chuckle. "But on land this time."

She nods again, and is silent for another moment before an apology tumbles from her. "I'm so sorry, Ben. I should have said something."

Not wanting her to feel one ounce of remorse over any time we spend together, including this disaster of a date, I slide closer and unbuckle her seat belt. I gather her in my arms and pull her into my lap and up against my chest. "No apologies. I understand you were only trying to brave it out to please me."

Her head bobs up and down against my shirt, her soft hair tickling the exposed portion of my chest. And, yes, I inhale again, because even though she was sick only a short time ago, she still smells fucking amazing.

"Will you give me a chance to redeem myself?" I whisper gently against the top of her head.

She nods again and snuggles her body into mine, resting her head against my shoulder. "I think I'm the one that needs to do the redeeming here."

"Dinner tomorrow? At my place? I'll cook for you, and I promise, I live on solid ground."

She nods again but then stops abruptly. "I actually have plans tomorrow night, but I can do the night after if you're free."

"I am now." I pull her petite frame tighter against me and

drop another kiss on top of her head. I hate that she's feeling so terrible and that it's my doing. I guess I'll have to make sure I do a little recon work for our next date—find out what she likes and doesn't like to eat, and any allergies she may have. I am not going to put her in a position again where she feels like she may disappoint me.

The car comes to a slow stop as it pulls up outside of her building. The driver jumps quickly out of the car and opens my door for me. Jill moves to get off my lap, but I move my arms under her legs and pull her flush to me. "I've got you."

I turn and place both feet on the pavement and thank God I've strengthened my one good leg so it's strong enough to rise out of the car with her in my arms. She looks up at me, her eyes soft, her color finally returning to the lovely shade of pink it should be, the corners of her perfect lips lifting just slightly. "Thank you for taking care of me, Benjamin."

What I really want to do is crush my mouth against hers, but instead, I brush a soft kiss against her forehead and smile. "Nothing gives me greater pleasure." And I truly mean it when I say it.

The door to her building opens before I even reach it, a look of concern on the doorman's face. "Is everything okay, Ms. Baldwin? Can I do anything?"

"Everything's fine. Just an upset stomach. Can you get the elevator for us?" I stride in its direction, the doorman scurrying ahead of me to push the call button.

"Ms. Baldwin, you just ring down if you need anything. James or myself will run out."

"You're so sweet, Henry. Thank you." She smiles weakly as we pass by and into the elevator that has arrived.

I nod my head in thanks to Henry, and then look at Jill. "You okay to stand? I'll put you down if so."

She nods her head, so I lower her legs to the floor but keep one arm firmly around her waist to keep her close. "What floor?"

"Penthouse."

My brows rise in surprise as I lean forward and stretch my hand out to push the PH button.

"It's not like that. Really. I share it with Mikaela Kingsley," she says defensively.

"I didn't say a thing." But now it all makes sense. Mikaela is filthy rich, and one of the sweetest women on the planet. I'm happy to know she's living in good company.

"I saw the look on your face when I said penthouse," she retorts.

Ah, she's definitely feeling better. Her spark is flickering back to life, and this makes me smile down at her in relief. "That was simply surprise. No judgement."

"Well, I hope not. I've worked really hard for what I have. Mik has been a godsend and one of my best friends."

Unable to help myself, I bend down and peck a kiss on the very tip of her nose. "I agree. Mikaela is one of the very best people I know."

This seems to placate her, because she just nods her head tightly and then leans against my shoulder. I wish I could hold her against me all night, but know I need to put her needs first. The elevator comes to a stop and we step out into the foyer.

There are two penthouse suites on the floor so I turn and look at her. "Which door?"

"Oh, sorry, that one." Her delicate hand snakes out from the blanket, and a finger points to the door on the left. I lead us in that direction and am about to ask her for the key, when the door swings open, Mikaela standing in the entrance.

"Jill! What happened?" She glances to her friend and then up at me with an accusatory expression on her face. "What did you do to her, Benjamin Sapphire?"

I'm about to speak my defense, but Jill beats me to it. "He's been wonderful, Mik. I just got a bit seasick."

Mik slaps my arm and then places her hands on her hips. "You took her on a boat? Are you crazy?"

I let out a sigh an in attempt to stay calm. "Can you step aside so we can come in?"

"Oh!" Her eyes pop wide as she realizes she's standing in the middle of the doorway and moves. "Sorry."

I lift one brow and frown as I walk past her, Jill still pressed to my side. "I had no idea she got seasick. She didn't tell me until *after* the boat left the shore and got sick."

I stop and turn my head toward a trailing Mik. "I would never have put her in a position to make her ill if I had known." I continue further into the apartment.

I look down at Jill and soften my voice. "Which way to your room Angel?"

She tilts her head to one side of the room. "Down that hallway. It's the second door on the left, but, Ben, I'm okay now. I'm feeling much better."

"I've got you." I don't care how uncomfortable she might

feel right now; I'm not letting her go until I know she's safe in her room.

I follow the direction she's given and guide her into the bedroom. Mik's still trailing behind me and flicks on the light, then runs around me so she can pull back the covers on the bed. I gently place Jill on the bed and slide my arm out from around her waist.

She smiles up at me and trails her hand down my arm as it moves away from her, finding my hand and giving it a squeeze. "Thank you, Ben. Even though things didn't go quite as planned, you've been wonderful."

I lean forward, wrap my free hand around the back of her head, and pull her forward until my lips press against her forehead in a quick kiss. "I promise, our next date will be one thousand times better."

"I can't wait," she whispers back.

We release each other as I rise and turn to find Mik watching us like a hawk. Before she can squawk at me again, I raise my finger to silence her. "Just take care of her."

I stroll past her and out of the apartment before she can say another word.

"Sure sounds like that date went well." Mikaela jests, amused as she sits on the bed next to me.

I dramatically bury my head into the pillow and groan loudly, much to her delight. "Glad that my misery is entertaining to you."

Mikaela pats me on the head. "I'm sorry, babe. I promise I'll try to wait and glee over your misery later when you feel better."

"Gee, thanks." I deadpan.

I stand and head to the bathroom so I can change and brush my teeth, but both our heads snap to the door, which is thrown open as Raeva bursts in. "What the heck happened?" she demands.

Rae looks incredible; dressed to the nines in a stunning gown. She and Mika must have been on a date themselves. That man is always thinking of ways to sweep her off her feet.

"Well?" she urges as she lowers herself on the bed with Mik, watching as I grab pajamas from a drawer and walk into my attached bathroom. I can hear them loud and clear as I change and brush my teeth.

"He took her on a yacht," Mikaela explains.

"Is he crazy?" Raeva belts out.

"My exact response to him."

Mikaela says, frowning, "When we got back from dinner and James told us that you were carried in the building looking like a ghost, I nearly had a conniption! I left Mika standing in the lobby and ran into the elevator!" She throws her hands up in the air, her head shaking. "Ugh, I could kill Ben right now! What the heck was he thinking?"

"He didn't know. It's not his fault," I protest as I walk back into the room. "I swear, guys, he was amazing. So sweet. He held my hair and stroked my back and practically carried me to the car. Ben really was the perfect gentleman."

I look up when there is a lack of response and find my two besties gaping at me.

"Jillian Baldwin, are you swooning?" Rae teases.

I roll my eyes.

"Don't deny it, you totally are." Mik chimes in.

I sigh. What's the point in denying? My flushed cheeks have already betrayed me. "He asked me out again," I admit reluctantly.

"Tell us everything," the say in unison. "And don't you dare leave anything out!"

I can't help the smirk that appears on my face when I start to talk about Ben. Up until the point that I started to hug the porcelain throne, it was a great date.

"Are you just going stare dreamily into space, or are you going to take us out of our misery and fill us in?" Rae prods.

"I mean, I have been sitting here all night waiting for you to come home!" Mik whines.

I roll my eyes in an attempt to mask my amusement.

"Did he kiss you? Or did you get sick before he had the chance?" Mik asks.

"Oh, he kissed me." I say with a sigh as I recall how his lips felt against mine.

The two of them squeal like school girls, and honestly, it's hard to resist the urge to join them. That kiss was amazing, and I'm pretty sure if the waitress on the boat hadn't interrupted us, I may have begun shedding my clothing right there on the deck; cold weather and seasickness be damned.

I share the details of the kiss with the girls, and they hang on my every word, sighing dreamily when I finish. As I recount the entire experience, I swear I can feel my lips tingle.

"Wow that sounds amazing. So, swoon worthy." Mikaela says, a soft smile on her lips.

"Yes, up until you started to expel your stomach's contents, it sounds like it was the perfect date." Rae agrees.

"I know, I know." I shake my head at my own mistake. "I should have told him that boats and I don't mix. But, you guys, I didn't want to come across as high maintenance! Though, in hind sight, I guess that probably would have been better than having him watch me throw my guts up." I state, mortified at the memory.

"I actually think it is romantic." Mik gushes.

"Come again?"

"Well, he took care of you Jillybean. He didn't leave you to your own devices. I'm not even sure if I could have stayed with you to watch you hurl."

I already know this, but hearing her say it out loud makes it even more real to me; Benjamin Sapphire is pretty special. And even though I've agreed to go on another date with him, I wasn't completely sure if I would actually go through with it.

Between the mortifying evening and my reservations about dating, I was seriously considering he might be better off without me. The one thing holding me back was that damn kiss. That scorching as hell, soak my panties, tongue stroking, I'm so damn fucked, kiss.

CHAPTER
Six

I've learned, after drilling Mik and Raeva, that Jill loves a good steak, french fries, and asparagus with hollandaise sauce. So, that's what's on the menu for tonight.

I've got the steak marinating, sides prepped, and a bottle of red already open to breathe. She's supposed to be here at 7:00, but knowing from our past meetings that she's always prompt, I expect she'll be arriving any minute.

While I don't live in a penthouse, I do live in a very nice loft. I had it renovated after I bought the building for the gym, which is located downstairs.

It's a large, open space that contains a restaurant-worthy industrial kitchen, a living space filled with a couple of couches, a large flat-screen television, and a bedroom in the back corner that I had sectioned off with some retro glass bricking. I've got rugs scattered throughout on the hardwood floors, and retractable blinds cover the very large warehouse windows that surround three of the outside walls.

I lit some candles, actually ran a vacuum over the floors, and made sure my bed had fresh sheets on it. I wasn't sure what direction our date was going to take, but I certainly hoped that it might end up in the bedroom.

I dressed comfortably, in a pair of worn jeans and a black t-shirt. Now, all I need is my date. No sooner than that thought crosses my mind, the bell to the elevator dings.

The beat of my heart ratchets up a few notches as I make my way over to the call button. I press it and speak. "Come on up."

I press another button that unlocks the elevator down below and hear the large doors clank shut and then some light rattling of the wires as it begins to rise.

My bare feet pace back and forth a few short steps, and then stop when the doors slide open revealing who I've come to believe is the most beautiful woman in the world.

She seems to have followed suit with my casual attire, because she's also wearing a pair of jeans; although, hers are much darker and fit snug over her long legs. She's got some kind of light cotton top on that's sitting off her shoulders, in a pretty teal color, and has a jacket over her arm.

She holds up a bottle of red wine and beams brightly. "I brought wine!"

I stroll toward her, take the bottle, and using my free hand, cup her face. I tug her just close enough to place a soft kiss against her cheek. "All I need is you."

She flushes a light pink and lets out a soft sigh as a small smile graces her lips. "Hi, Ben."

"Hi." I release her and swing my hand over the space in front of us. "Welcome. Not a single wave in sight."

She chuckles and runs a hand down her face to hide her embarrassment. "Ugh. Let's forget about that disaster. Please!"

"Done." I take her hand in mine and start toward the kitchen. "You look beautiful, by the way."

"I feel like I should take my heels off so we're on even ground." She giggles beside me.

"Angel, we ain't ever gonna be on even ground. You're always going to be floating in a space much higher than me." I turn and slide my gaze down her body. "No matter what you're wearing."

She tucks her chin in as she tries to hide the blush coloring her cheeks. "Ben, you have to stop saying things like that to me."

We reach the kitchen, so I place the bottle of wine on the island and turn, yanking her up against me by our joined hands, a small gasp of surprise coming from her as our bodies crash together.

I place a finger under her chin and raise it until I'm gazing into her eyes. "I don't know how other men have treated you, but you deserve to be told every day how goddamn beautiful you are. Every time I see you, you take my breath away." I give a small shake of my head. "I don't know how you do it, but each time I see you, you're even more gorgeous than the time before."

Her lips form a small 'o' shape, as her eyes grow wide.

"So, if you're going to be with me, get used to hearing it. You're fucking stunning. A literal angel walking on this earth. I'd almost bet you have wings hidden under that shirt if I didn't already see your bare back the night of the opening."

Her fingers, which were clutched around my biceps a moment ago, have started to trail gently down my arms as something in her gaze shifts. I watch as her tongue darts out to swipe across her lips, leaving them wet and shiny, causing my restraint to finally snap. My hands move up the back of her neck, sliding around to capture her face, and then I crash my lips to hers.

It's not the first time I've kissed her, but it's the first time I've had sparks light up under my eyelids as the heat of her breath mixes with mine when our mouths fuse together. She groans, and I take advantage, sliding my tongue against hers, deepening our kiss.

Her fingernails dig into my arms where she's clutching them, her body pressing more tightly against mine. I know she's discovered the growing bulge below my waist when she rubs her core up and down my length, another small moan vibrating against my mouth.

I move my hands to clutch under her ass and lift, urging her to wrap her legs around me, and begin walking blindly toward my bedroom. Her hands are gripping my hair as she tries to control the heat of our kiss, her lips breaking away from me as they begin to nip down my neck. My head falls back, a low growl rolling from my chest as she latches on and sucks hard for just a second before releasing and moving lower.

My fingers dig into her ass as I yank her tighter against my now fully erect cock, her mouth leaving my skin as her head raises, her gaze locking onto mine, eyes wild with desire. My knees hit the bed at the same time, and I lower her back onto the bed, my body hovering just inches above hers.

"Are we really doing this?" Her question comes out breathy.

I can't believe I'm lying here, on my back, in his bed, and it's only our second date. And it's not because I don't want to be here, I do. So badly. He runs his nose along my neck and across my cheek before he plunges his mouth on mine once more. Our tongues dance furiously with each other, stirring the flame of our desire higher.

He pulls back and captures my gaze with his. "Is it too soon?" he pants out in response to my question.

His genuine concern for me, and the fact that he seems to actually be asking my permission instead of talking me into something I might not want, makes the decision easy for me. I shake my head. "If it is, I don't care." Truer words have never been spoken by me.

Ben reacts by grinding his enormous length against my core, and I nearly combust on the spot. Our mouths fuse together once more, more frantic than moments ago when I would have sworn we could not feel more heat.

Both of us are wearing too many clothes right now, so I slide my hands down his back until I find the hem of his shirt, grasp it in my fingers and start pulling it up to take it off. When he realizes, his lips break away from mine long enough to assist me with the process before slamming back home. My nails dig deep into his back as I grind up against him, needing him urgently.

Ben shifts away from me and yanks me to a sitting position. I watch as his fingers skim down over my breasts until they find the hem of my shirt, which he bunches in his fingers and then lifts over my head. I automatically raise my arms as he does and shiver in delight when he takes my smaller hands in one of his larger ones and pushes me back on the bed.

"Stay right there." He orders, and it's so entirely sexy that even the little rebel on my shoulder nods her head obediently.

I suck my bottom lip between my teeth and bite down, welcoming the sting of it. Ben's gaze slides to my mouth, growling fiercely as he lowers his mouth onto my shoulder and starts peppers kisses in a line straight to my breasts.

His mouth finds my nipple over my bra, which isn't difficult since they are currently hard as rocks, and draws it into his mouth with a sharp pull. My hips jerk up into his, once again rubbing against his swollen center, and I moan loudly. He smirks briefly before moving to the other side, giving my other nipple the same attention.

My bra has a front clasp, and he seems to have no issue snapping it open. His strong hands slide the fabric off and grasp onto each breast, and I nearly scream out when he squeezes.

I can't help the moan that falls from my lips; it's loud and needy. I want his mouth back on my breasts, and I have no trouble letting him know. I grip his hair in both hands and force him back in their direction. He chuckles but obliges none the less. His tongue circles around my nipple before he sucks on it, hard. My body jumps in response. "Oh my God. Yes, Ben!"

He moves to the other breast, eliciting the same response, before finally making his way down, lower, where I am literally aching for him. I am throbbing between my thighs. His mouth finds the button of my jeans, and I almost come when the man rips them open with his teeth! *Holy fuck, that is hot.*

He grips the waistband of the denim fabric and slides it off me with remarkable skill. In my dazed state, it takes me a moment to realize that my panties are coming down as well. I have no objections, and in compliance, lift my hips, making the process easier and faster. As my need for him grows to epic proportions, my patience dwindles at the same rate. In an effort to assist him in ridding me of my jeans and panties, I push at the back of my heels with my toes to release my shoes. They fall onto the floor with a loud thud, and then I am completely naked, entirely exposed to him. Both physically and emotionally.

Every wall has come down, and I want to join my body with his more than I want to take my next breath. He leans back over me, but he is still entirely too dressed, and I want him naked. "Uh-uh. I want yours off, too."

My hands move to his top button and tug it free. My eyes flicker to his, and I think I see him hesitate for just a moment before he tugs at the zipper and pushes his jeans down off his legs. When he is fully naked, I swallow hard. I felt him grind up against me before, and I knew he was… large, but Jesus, his cock is huge! He's going to destroy my pussy. I relish the idea. My eyes flicker a little lower, and I remember the prosthetic now that I have my eyes on it. I get it now; the slight hesitation.

"Do you need to take it off?" I nod my head in it's direction.

It's the first time I've seen his confidence stutter, his cheeks flushing just the slightest pink. "Do you mind? It's actually easier if I do, and more comfortable."

Shit, all I want is for him to screw my brains out. I catch his gaze and make sure he can see the look in my eyes when I tell him, "Ben, just do whatever you need to do to fuck me already."

His face lights up at my blunt reply, and he shakes his head slightly, as if he cannot believe the words that have just fallen from my lips. He sits up and pulls the prosthetic off with lightning speed, and before I can even blink, he's on top of me, caging me with an arm on either side. I take advantage of this position and allow my hands to explore that magnificent painted chest of his, gliding my fingers over the perfection above me. But hunger soon overtakes me. I need his mouth on mine. I have never been known for my patience, and I am not about to start now. I pull him down until his lips crash onto mine.

His swollen head is sliding against the throbbing between my thighs, now soaked with my need. I move my hips up and down to show him just how ready I am for him. He reaches over to the bedside table and pulls out a condom, rolling onto his side to slide it on.

He is taking too long; I don't want to wait another second, so I push him onto his back and straddle him. He looks up at me with wide eyes, his lips curled up in surprise. I lower my pussy against his length and glide over it back and forth, the pressure against my clit pure heaven.

He says something, but I am too lost in my nirvana to even comprehend words. I'm done waiting and move to position myself over him before driving him into me in one push. I welcome the sting, screaming out my relief as his impressive length impales me. "Yes!"

I rise up until he's almost out of me and drop down again, adjusting to his magnificent cock more quickly this time. Ben thrusts up at the same time and leaves me feeling so impossibly full that I think he's going to split me in two. We move in perfect sync, as if this was rehearsed a million times and we are competing for finals. I fall into ecstasy as the muscles in my core begin to tighten around his cock.

Tingles run across every inch of my skin, and I close my eyes as my orgasm starts to crest. I rock myself harder against Ben and moan as I pulse around him in such welcome relief. Just when I think it's over, he rolls me onto my back and starts to pump into me even more deeply than before.

I wrap my legs around him, locking him against me, meeting each of his thrusts with a loud grunt. His arms tighten around me as I crest yet again, a second orgasm exploding from me as I scream his name out. He thrusts one final time, hard and deep, his head thrown back as he bellows out my name, his cock jerking inside of me with his release.

We both lay panting for a moment before he rolls over, his semi-erect cock sliding out of me as he does. and then pulls me close. He wraps his arms around me, tugging me flush to him, kissing the top of my head. "That was fucking amazing," he says, out of breath.

"Yeah, it wasn't too bad," I say, like the smart ass I am.

He lifts his head to look down at me, brow arched. "Not too bad?"

I shrug against him. "Well, I usually at least get dinner when I'm on a date." I smirk as I trace my fingers lazily over his chest.

"Oh, honey, this date is just getting started. I'm going to make you dinner, and then we're going to do this all over again. But better."

"It gets better?"

"For someone who just said it wasn't too bad, I think I'm going to have to do whatever I can to make sure it gets better." He flashes me his most devilish smile.

Yep, now I am quite literally fucked. But damn, did that feel good.

CHAPTER
Seven

I've slept with my fair share of women over the years. But fuck me, I don't think I've ever felt this satisfied. Ever.

I haven't even scratched the surface with what I want to do to this woman. This was hard and fast and full of desperation, but I still need to explore every inch of Jill's delicious body.

I want to do it right now, in fact, but my date has requested I feed her, so feed her I will… more than my cock. I chuckle at my own internal joke and shift my gaze as her fingers stop trailing over my stomach then lay flat as she pushes to lean up and look at me.

"What's so funny?" One brow is raised over her gorgeous gray eyes.

The side of my mouth rises in a cocky grin before I lean forward and press my lips against hers. "Just wondering how I got lucky enough to get your gorgeous ass in my bed."

"Trying to distract me with compliments?" She grins back down at me.

"Oh, if I was going to distract you, I would do something like this." Before she can react, I roll her over and capture her lips in mine, slide a hand over her breast, and gently roll her taut nipple between my fingers. Her mouth opens as a soft moan falls from her lips, and I sweep my tongue inside, loving the feeling of her breath against mine. I kiss her for only a minute, making sure to leave her wanting, and then pull slowly away. "Didn't you say something about me feeding you?"

Her hands snake up and latch onto the longer locks of my hair as she pulls my face close to hers. "I've said it once, Benjamin Sapphire, but I'll say it again. You, sir, are a tease."

I grin salaciously. "Me?"

"Yes. You." She draws my face forward until it's only a hair's breadth from hers and then darts her tongue out, sliding it across my lips in one slow motion. I inhale deeply and force myself to keep my head still instead of crashing my mouth onto hers like I desire. "Just don't forget that two can play at this game."

"I like when you're feisty." I snake my own tongue out and trace it over my lips, following the same path hers did. "But you're right. Let's eat first. I want to make sure you have enough energy for what I'm planning to do to you later."

Her eyes widen, and I feel her body shift under me as her cheeks flush a stunning shade of pink. "I think I can live with that plan."

I lower myself the tiny fraction required and place a soft

kiss on her lips before pushing myself up and off her. Her eyes roam down my chest so I look down in question and then back at her. "Too much?" I have a lot of ink. I don't see a single mark on her body.

She shakes her head. "No." Her fingers reach out and graze over the wings of the phoenix on my shoulder. "I want to trace every single line with my tongue. It's incredibly sexy." Her eyes shift to meet mine. "You're incredibly sexy."

My fucking heart skips a beat, then another, and then another. I want to throw her back on this bed right now, shove my cock into her, and claim her as mine. Instead, I muster every ounce of will power I have and push my animalistic needs away for the moment. "You just may be the most perfect woman I've ever met, Jill Baldwin."

Her eyes grow wide for just a second before she blushes and shifts her gaze to her lap. I honestly don't think she's used to receiving compliments, which staggers me because she is truly the most gorgeous and humble woman I can ever remember meeting. Not wanting to embarrass her further, I shift to the end of the bed and move to place my prosthetic back on. I look over my shoulder as I do to address her. "Ready for some dinner? I'm going to make you the best steak you've ever had."

Her face lights up as she smiles and hops out of the bed. "Yes! I'm starving." She wiggles her eyebrows and smiles even brighter. "Plus, word on the street is that I'm going to need some extra fortitude for the rest of the evening."

She reaches down, plucks the t-shirt I had on earlier off

the floor, and yanks it over her head. I watch as she finds her panties and slides them up her legs.

Did I say she couldn't get any more beautiful? *Fuck me. I was wrong.* Seeing her in my shirt may be the hottest goddamn thing I've ever seen in my life. I rise off the bed, walk over, and draw her into my arms mumbling into her soft waves, "Where in the hell have you been hiding?"

Her arms tighten around me in response, clinging to me for a full minute before she loosens her grip to step away, her eyes meeting mine with a smile. "I guess good things are worth waiting for."

fter I pull on a pair of shorts, and no shirt per her request, we head to the kitchen and work together to cook dinner. I'm pleasantly surprised to learn she's an amazing cook and gives me some great tips on how to grill the asparagus, rather than steam it, for optimal flavor. As soon as I sink my teeth into the tender green stalks and the smoky flavor bursts in my mouth, I moan. Out loud. It's that good. Not a single drop of the hollandaise is needed, not that it stops her from dipping every bite in the delicious sauce.

I love that this woman eats with gusto. She wanted her steak rare and her fries crunchy, and I smile as she devours every morsel without apology. Seriously, this woman just keeps getting better and better.

Even though I made promises to have her for dessert,

after cleaning up the dinner dishes, we wander over to the big couches in the middle of my living space. We fold into one with full glasses of the wine I opened early, continuing the easy conversation that's been flowing between us. She curls her legs underneath her like a cat, her long bare limbs exposed past her thighs where my t-shirt sits.

"So, tell me all the things I don't know about you yet, Ben." Her lips kiss the edge of her glass as she takes a sip of the dark red liquid, her eyes locked on me.

"Tell me what you know and I'll fill in the blanks," I counter, not smugly but challengingly.

She tilts her head in acceptance. "Well, I know you're a Sapphire, which basically means you're rich."

I shrug my shoulders. It's not something I can deny. I was lucky enough to be born to a father who worked his ass off to build an empire. Now, Drew and I run it, and we're able to enjoy and reap the benefits of its success. "Does it bother you that I'm rich?"

She shakes her head back and forth. "No, because you don't act like you are. You could choose to do whatever you like, live wherever you want, but instead, you live in a loft. You joined the Army. And look what you've done downstairs. I mean, could you be any more selfless?"

I look down into my glass and think about how to respond to this, because I think, initially, when I started the gym, it was purely for selfish reasons. I decide to be honest and share this with her. "I'm not quite the savior you paint me to be, Jill. When I lost my leg, I went to a really dark place. I almost got lost there and may not have made it back if it wasn't for my stubborn brother and another really stubborn physical therapist at the hospital."

She shifts closer to me and, completely astonishing me, places her hand on the seam where my prosthetic meets my scarred leg. "This happened in the war?"

I'm not lying when I tell you that not a single person, outside of medical staff, has ever touched my wound. Her touch shifts something inside of me, making me aware of how special this woman is.

Emotion threatens to steal my voice, so I clear my throat as I try to shake it away. "Yes. Our truck hit an IED." I stop to look at her and clarify in case she doesn't understand. "An explosive buried in the ground."

She nods, so I continue before I lose my nerve. "It was bad. Really bad. When I woke up, I just remember seeing blood everywhere, and body parts, and feeling terrified when I looked down and saw how mangled my leg was. But it was nothing compared to looking beside me and seeing one of my best friends dead."

I stop then because the old anger of being the one to survive, of being alive when two of my friends are dead, is boiling under the surface. She doesn't need to see that. And, again, I'm astonished when she moves even closer and takes my hand in hers, squeezing gently. "I'm so, so sorry for your losses, Ben. I can't begin to comprehend what you must have suffered, but I'm really glad your stubborn brother saw you through."

Blinking rapidly to damn the emotion that's trying to break free behind my lids, I shake my head again in wonder. I clear my throat again and continue my story. "So, you see,

I needed to do something with all that anger. Once I could stand on my own again."

I release her hand for only a moment to knock on my leg to expand on my statement, and then take it back in mine, "I found a way to release some of it and began boxing. When I left the hospital, I wanted a space more private where I didn't feel like everyone was looking at my leg, or if I lost my balance and fell, I didn't have people feeling sorry for me."

I shrug, regarding the space around me. "I bought this building and initially just put a punching bag in. Then I invited some of my brothers, and then they invited some more, and the next thing I knew, I had a full-fledged gym. It would have been selfish of me not to open the doors to other men like me who needed a place to go and didn't have it." I glance over to find her staring at me intently.

She finally graces me with a smile as she moves her head back and forth in a slow motion. "Do you understand how amazing what you've done is? I'm in awe of you, Ben, complete awe."

I stare into my glass and then take a sip of wine before replying. I'm embarrassed. I did this for me, and being able to help my other brothers-in-need just happened naturally, not because of anything I did consciously. "Don't be. Be in awe of the men and women who are still out there fighting and protecting us. And for the families here waiting with baited breath for them to come home. They are the ones to admire." I shake my head firmly. "Not me."

She scoots even closer to me, and I wonder if she's going to climb into my lap, but instead, she grasps my chin between her tiny fingers and pulls my face in her direction. "That is what makes what you've done so amazing. You take no credit for how much you help these people and feel less for doing it. That makes you one of the most giving men, and maybe, I'm now proud to say, one of the most admired men I have ever had the honor of knowing."

I'm stunned by her words and at a loss as to how to respond to them, so I lean forward and press my lips to hers. Her hand moves from my chin and slides around my neck to deepen the kiss, but it doesn't take a passionate turn. This kiss is different; it's filled with feelings I've never experienced and leaves me breathless with its meaning. Before I can think about it further, she draws back, places a kiss to my nose, and then slides down to curl into my body.

"Okay, so we've got rich, one-legged, selfless, and amazing kisser out of the way. What else should I know about you, Ben?"

I laugh out loud and pull her closer to me as I do, enjoying the feeling of her warm body pressed into mine. I tell her about my sister that died in a car accident at sixteen, how hard it was for my family, how much my brother Drew, although younger, has really always taken care of me. I tell her how we spent our summers in Northern California on the beach, surfing, playing football, and chasing girls. I tell her how much I love Hannah and the children she's brought into our lives and how they brought my parents back to life.

We talk for hours, her also sharing her story with me, until we finally grow quiet and just sit in each other's company. Sometime during the night, or early hours of the morning, we both drift to sleep on the couch, her safely encased in my arms. As her soft breaths whisper against my bare chest, my heart is fuller than it's ever felt before.

My eyes flutter open as little rays of sunshine dance across my face. Ben's arm is draped over me, and I can hear the steady beat of his heart under my cheek. A warmth spreads through me and my lips curl into a smile. I squeeze my eyes shut again, trying to keep reality at bay for just a little longer.

I inhale his scent, a faint trace of his cologne mixed with my perfume. The scents compliment each other perfectly. I focus on his breathing, and everything inside of me just wants to sneak a peek at him while he's sleeping.

I carefully slip out from the warmth of his arms and park my backside on top of the coffee table and just stare at him. The cold surface under my barely covered ass bothers me at first, but is quickly forgotten as I admire him. He's sleeping peacefully and smiling contently while doing so.

I stare at him a little while longer, watching his gorgeous chest rise and fall. As I study his tattoos, I resist the urge to touch them, to trace them with my fingers. I feel my heart rate accelerate, and the butterflies are back. *There they are again.*

I blink. And then I blink again. My hand raises to cover my now open mouth.

"No," I whisper.

My eyes widen when realization hits me. I am falling for him—hard. *I am fucking falling for Benjamin Sapphire.*

Suddenly, the butterflies make way for feelings of doom. Panic seizes around my throat. The little nagging voice in the back of my head tells me that a man like Ben doesn't stick around for the long run, and here I am stupid enough to let myself fall for him.

He makes a little growling noise, and it startles me. He turns over, and I release the breath I didn't know I was holding. I have to get out of here. I know I am going to need to wear more than Ben's shirt to get home, so I stealthily get up and tiptoe to his bedroom.

I gather my clothing, which is scattered all across the room, and shrug into my jeans. I pull Ben's shirt off, which still smells of him. I can't stop myself from bringing it to my nose a final time to inhale his scent before placing it on his bed. With my own top back on, I find my heels at the foot of the bed.

I don't put them on yet. I don't want the clicking to wake Ben. I go in search of my jacket, knowing that my cell phone is in the pocket. I don't have to look far; it's hanging on a hook near the entrance.

I press the elevator button and am relieved when the doors slide open. I step into the elevator, press the button to go to the lobby and slip my heels on my feet, my heart beating in my throat.

I'm grateful I didn't wake him. I cannot bear the thought of an awkward goodbye. He got me in his bed, like he wanted, and now it's done. And that's okay.

Ugh, that's a lie. It meant so much more to me, but I

need to cut this off before I get in too deep. If I am falling for this man already, after just a couple dates, what will I feel like in another couple weeks when he's ready for something new? And I guy like Ben always wants something fresh and new.

"I've made the right decision," I tell myself as the doors slide closed.

When I get out of the cab, Rae is standing at the curb with some cash in her hand. Mikaela is pacing behind her. I didn't take my purse to Ben's last night, and I had no money for the cab I hailed. Tears burn behind my eyelids when I see my two besties. I sent a 911 text on my way back and here they are. No questions asked, they are just here.

Raeva hands the cabby the cash and tells him to keep the change. She turns toward me and must see the look on my face because she immediately pulls me into an embrace.

That's when the dam breaks. In the middle of the street, in the brisk New York City morning air. While hordes of people buzz around us.

"Awe, honey. Shhhh," she says as she ushers me into our building.

Mikaela has walked ahead of us and called for the elevator. We walk into it, and when the doors slide to a close, I realize that for the first time since I moved in to the building, I didn't even greet the doorman. I'm not sure why I am focusing on that right now. We ride up to the penthouse, but nobody says a word. The elevator is filled with echoes of my not so silent sobbing.

I'm not sure why I am crying like this; I feel ridiculous. After all, I am the one who snuck out of Ben's place. I am the one who allowed myself to start falling for him, and I am the one who fell into bed with him.

The elevator door opens, and we step into the hallway just as Mika is stepping out of their penthouse. I use my sleeve as a makeshift hanky and wipe my eyes. When his gaze lands on me, his brow shoots up and his eyes flicker from his wife to his sister before landing back on me again.

"Everything okay?" he asks.

Raeva strolls toward him and gets on her tiptoes to plant a kiss on his lips. "Yes, baby. Just girl stuff."

He looks at me and gives me a half-smile and a nod. "Okay then, I'll leave you ladies to it then."

Mika kisses his wife and walks over to kiss his sister's cheek. Then he stops in front of me and places his hand on my shoulder. "I'm not sure what is going on, but whatever you need, I'm here." Then he leans in and kisses my cheek as well.

I smile weakly at him as I thank him, but I am genuinely grateful, because I know he means it. With that, Mika steps into the elevator, and we turn and step into our penthouse. We head straight for the living area where I curl up the couch, the girls following suit.

"So, Jillybean, what happened?" Rae asks.

"Did he hurt you?" Mik inquires at the same time.

"No."

My two friends share a look.

"You had sex and it was terrible?" Raeva says as she wrinkles her nose.

"Oh, God no. I mean, we had sex. In fact, it may have been some of the best sex of my life."

Rae looks at me skeptically.

"I swear. Ben is great. Last night was amazing."

The two of them look at me with brows furrowed.

"What's the problem then?" Mik questions.

I sigh. "I like him."

Mikaela frowns, but Raeva's expression displays an understanding."You like him and you're running," she says, matter of factly.

I nod once more. "But it's not as simple as that, guys. I am a realist. This thing was never going to work out. Sure, Ben likes me just fine. Now. But he is not the settling down kind of guy."

I arch a brow and stare at them both. "You both know his reputation as well as I do. He's a man about town and makes no secrets about it."

Raeva shakes her head. "So, you're not even going to give him a chance to fall in love with you?" She cocks her head like this should be so obvious. "Because you know he will, right?"

"I live in the real world, Rae." I lift my mouth in a forced smile. "And this girl would rather walk away now, before I get burned."

"But what if you're wrong?" Mik challenges. "What if he wants more? Isn't what you're feeling worth taking the chance?"

I frown. "My instincts are telling me to cut and run before I get hurt."

"Listen, you can still change your mind. You snuck out? He doesn't need to know you did. We can always tell him that you had an early meeting and didn't want to wake him?" Mik continues, still trying to convince me that I've made a mistake.

I shake my head. "No, I can't see him again."

"Jilly—"

"No, I mean it," I interrupt sternly.

They both hold up their hands.

"Listen, I know it's hard for you guys to understand, but I am doing this to protect myself. I just can't risk him breaking my heart. I know he doesn't intend to, but that is where this will end—in heart break." I sigh. "Besides, I am doing business with them. I should have never mixed business with pleasure."

My besties share another look, and I know that they are skeptical. But, never the less, they pull me into a group hug.

"If that's what you want, we support you," Mik tells me.

There is a knock on the front door, and the three of us look at each other. It's barely after 9:00 am, so no one we know would be knocking this early. Mikaela rises to her feet and goes to answer.

Rae and I duck down on the couch and peek over it as she opens the door. We both chuckle when we see it's one of the doormen. He hands her an enormous bouquet of white lilies then shuts the door for her.

Of course, I already know who they're from. My stomach knots up as Mik approaches me. She places the flowers on the coffee table and plucks out the card. She holds it out for me, but I shake my head. I can't bring myself to read it because I know that the words will be perfect and that my resolve will weaken the moment I do.

"Are you sure?" she asks.

I swallow hard, press my lips tightly together, and nod my head.

"Do you want to keep the flowers?"

I can't look at them without feeling an ache in my chest, so I shake my head. She nods thoughtfully, proceeds to pick up the flowers, and walks toward the kitchen.

Rae scoots over to me to wrap her arms around me. She pulls me closer and hugs me from the side. "Honey, I can't say that I understand your reasoning, or even that I agree with it. But I support whatever it is that you want, okay?"

I lay my head on her shoulder and nod.

Told you I'd be screwed.

Eight

It's been three days since I woke on my couch to find my arms empty and Jill gone. Three days of unanswered texts and phone calls. Three days that I've sent numerous bouquets of her favorite flowers to both her office and her penthouse.

Two days of calls to Mikaela, demanding she tell me what's wrong with Jill, and still no answers, only evasion. Mikaela says she's extremely busy working and hasn't seen her to even speak with her. Fucking girl code. I know without a doubt Mikaela's covering for her.

What I don't understand is what the hell happened between her falling asleep in my arms and waking up the next morning alone. The night we spent together was one of the best of my life. I have never felt a connection like the one I do with her. There is no way I am letting her run away from me now.

I punch the bag in front of me one more time for good

measure and then lean my exhausted body against it in defeat. I've been punching the shit out of it for the last two hours, and my knuckles are red and swollen. I'm surprised they haven't bled out under the tape yet.

I'm going crazy waiting for some kind of message from her and am at my wit's end over what I should do next. Letting out a tired breath, I push myself off the bag and head toward the shower.

After rinsing off two hours of sweat in steaming hot water, I change into a pair of jeans and a hoodie. I decide to go see the one person who might understand more than anyone what it's like when the woman you crave just disappears.

Leaving the building, I walk outside into the crisp fall air. It's days like this that I wish I could still ride my bike. I've talked to some guys that have had their bikes modified to allow them to be able to ride again, but I just haven't gotten that far yet.

Instead, I walk into the alley beside my building and slide into my Dodge Charger. It's a badass car and makes up for the fact that I can't swing my leg over a bike on afternoons like this.

I put the key in the ignition and turn it, the engine roaring to life, and for good measure, I press on the gas, revving it loudly before I shift into reverse and out into traffic.

I'm in front of our hotel on Park Avenue in twenty minutes and hand the keys to the valet driver who greets me by name as I exit the vehicle. "Keep it close. I won't be long."

"Yes, sir." He doesn't give me a tag. He knows who I am. Being a Sapphire definitely has its perks.

I stroll through the lobby of the hotel to the elevator and press the floor number for his office. The elevator glides to its destination in seconds, and the doors swish open for me to exit. I stride down the hallway and smile at Felicia, sitting at her desk outside the large dual-office doors of my destination.

"Mr. Sapphire!" She smiles and exclaims in surprise. "Is the other Mr. Sapphire expecting you?"

I stop short of her desk and grimace. "Felicia, please, for the hundredth time, just call me Ben."

"Oh no! I could never do that, Mr. Sapphire." She shakes her head so hard you would think I just asked her to crawl across the floor on her hands and knees and lick the dirt off my boots.

"Really, you can. Actually, I insist." I watch as her eyes pop wide in shock at my order. "Just call me Ben. Mr. Sapphire is my father and makes me feel old."

"Okay, um, Ben." Her face turns an extremely dark shade of pink as she says my name, and I can't help the smile that forms on my lips. It's the first time it's happened in days. "The other Mr. Sapphire," she lowers her voice to a whisper, "Drew," she continues uncomfortably, pointing to his office doors, "he's in. He's alone, so you can just go in."

It's strange, but I just want to give her a hug to let her know that her protection of my brother, and her need to show us so much respect, doesn't go unnoticed and is appreciated. But, of course, I don't. I can only imagine what color she would turn then. Instead, I gently pat her hand as I thank her and then move past to knock on the door.

I don't bother waiting for an answer as I enter. Drew's attention shifts from his computer, a look of surprise and then subtle annoyance crossing his face as it lands on mine.

"Ah, I should have known. Only you enter unannounced, Benny Boy." He leans back in his chair and shakes his head, steepling his fingers in front of him as he does. "I was wondering when you'd show up."

I cock my head as I plop myself into one of the leather chairs in front of his desk. "Why's that?"

"Jill Baldwin's disappearing act?" he counters smugly.

"How the fuck do you know about that? I haven't talked to you in almost a week." I sit up straighter in the chair, anxious to see what information he has.

"Oh, I'm not supposed to know a thing." His brows raise. "And, believe me, I wish I didn't. But those women had a little hen session the other day, and it's all I've heard Hannah talk about since."

I widen my eyes and wave my hands in exasperation. "Well, what the fuck is going on?"

"Apparently, Jill had some kind of melt down about how she may or may not be feeling about you and has gone into retreat mode." He shrugs his shoulders.

"What the fuck does that mean? Retreat mode?" I question hotly.

"Jesus, I don't know, Ben." He runs his fingers through his hair and blows out a breath. "She's been burnt pretty badly in the past by a couple of men. Not just one, from what Hannah says. I think she's cagey about trusting or caring for anyone again."

I shake my head in frustration. "Drew, I've been nothing but a perfect gentleman to this woman. Done everything I can to assure her I'm on the level here. I mean, I shared shit with her that I've never shared with anyone. Not even you."

I flinch as I see an expression of hurt slide over his face and then just as quickly disappear, and groan inwardly that I've offended him. I continue in an effort to try to explain my way back into his good graces. "It's just different with her. Even though we haven't spent a lot of time together, I feel like my soul has known her forever. She's awakened something in me."

"Look, I get it, Ben. I was there with Hannah." He chuckles as his eyes roll back in memory. "And you know how hard it was to get her to see me and believe she wasn't wrong for doing so."

"So, what the hell am I supposed to do now? Not see her? Sit around and wait? Not being able to talk to her to try and fix this is driving me crazy." I stand and walk to the large window behind my brother and stare down at the park entrance below.

"Go find her, man." He rises and comes to stand next to me. "Funny story." He points to a bench sitting just to the left of the entrance. "When I thought I had completely lost Hannah, I found her sitting in the pouring rain, right there. My destiny was sitting right outside, and all I had to do was go down and make her mine."

I look over at him, my brows creased. "What the fuck is your point, Drew?"

He rolls his eyes and slaps a hand on my shoulder. "You don't have to wait for her to show up, Benny. You know where to find her. Go get her."

"Yeah? Just like that? Go invade her space?"

"Yeah. Just like that." His hand grips around my arm and shoves me in the direction of the door. "What the hell are you waiting for? You've got nothing to lose, right?"

I tilt my head, shrug my shoulders, and meet my brother's challenging look. "If this makes things worse, I'm gonna come back here and kick your ass, little brother."

"You can come and give it your best shot. Now, get the hell out of my office." He scoffs and points to the door.

Ten minutes later, I'm back in my car and headed to Serenity. My gut tells me that's where I'll find her. She's completely invested in her company, and I'm guessing she's buried herself in work. I'm not sure what I'm going to say when I see her, but I pray, when she does come face to face with me, she'll tell me what the fuck is wrong.

Another fifteen minutes later, I pull into a parking garage a block from the spa and then quickly walk the distance to its entrance. It's after four, and the waiting room is empty and quiet. I'm assuming they are probably done taking appointments today, and most likely in the process of finishing up whatever clients may still be in-house. No one's at the front desk, so I take a seat in the lobby and wait for someone to appear.

I pick up a magazine on the table and begin absently flipping through the pages when I hear voices around the corner. I go on high alert and stand, tip-toeing a bit closer when I hear Jill's name being spoken in the conversation.

"Yes, that guy, the tattooed one with the missing leg!"

They both giggle and shush each other at the same time.

"Well, from what I heard, what he's missing from one leg, he makes up with another. If you know what I mean!"

Another round of giggles ensues, and I roll my eyes at their immaturity. Really, they're gossiping about my dick? My irritation comes to a screeching halt when I hear Jill's name again.

"Anyway, I heard Jill tell Maria that if he comes in here again that she wants nothing to do with him. Maria can handle any and all business with him."

"But why? One leg or not, the guy is smoking hot."

"Something about having had enough damaged goods in her life and doesn't need anymore."

My heart lurches in my chest, and the blood in my veins turns icy cold as it races through my body, every inch of my skin hardening at what I just heard. *She thinks I'm damaged goods?* I shake my head in disbelief. She seemed totally fine with me, and my leg, the other night. Was it all an act? I can't stand to listen to another word these women are whispering.

I take a step backward and move to spin around and slam right into a side-table, the potted plant on it smashing to the ground. *Fuck me and my goddamn leg that doesn't feel a thing!*

Before I can escape, the gossiping girls appear from around the corner, their expressions changing from wonder to shock as they recognize me. I'm quite sure, based on the expression on both of their faces, they realize I just heard every word they've said.

They both begin apologizing and move to help with the plant, but I place my hand out flat. "Just stop." They comply instantly and freeze. Without another word to them, I spin on my good heel and leave the building as quickly as I arrived.

My blood, moments ago cold as ice from the words I overheard between the two women at the spa, is now flowing like lava under my skin as my rage grows. *Damaged fucking goods?*

I shake my head in disgust. Not at her, but at myself. For believing that a woman like Jill saw past my disability to see the man that I am. Who the hell was I kidding? Pieces of me are missing. A woman like her deserves someone whole.

I reach my car and yank the door open, throwing myself behind the driver's seat. I stare at the concrete wall in front of me and have a sudden urge to start the engine, put the car in reverse, and then plow forward until I smash head-on into its hard surface. Closing my eyes, I shake my head again. I haven't had dark thoughts like these in a very long time. If caring for a woman drives me to thoughts like this, maybe her not wanting me is for the best.

Banging my hands on the steering wheel, I let out a roar of frustration. It doesn't help relieve one bit of the pain that now seems to be clenching my heart. How is it possible after knowing this woman for only a few short weeks that I could feel so thoroughly gutted?

I lay my head on the steering wheel in defeat, already knowing the answer to my own question but trying in vain to push it to the recesses of my mind. I need to force her and whatever I was feeling to the very back corner of my heart and forget about her. Forget her smile, the silkiness of her skin under my fingers, her fresh rain scent, the way she felt under me, and especially how it felt when she trailed her fingers over me.

I lift my head to try to shake it clear. Darkness creeps in along the edges of my brain, and I know I need to move before it takes over completely. I start the car and exit the garage, paying the attendant as I do. I drive aimlessly for an hour and then head back to the hotel. Grabbing my cell phone off the passenger seat, I tell Siri to call Drew. Seconds later, his voice sounds on the other end.

"Benny, how'd it go?" He's upbeat and eager to hear my news, but I'm in no mood for small talk.

"Meet me at the bar in ten." I hit end without waiting for a response. I'm sure that alone will tell him what he needs to know.

Traffic is heavier now, so it's another fifteen minutes before I walk in and see him sitting at the far end. He's got a drink in his hand and another waiting on the bar in front of the stool beside him. I slide onto it, grab what I know will be whiskey, and drink it in two long gulps. He doesn't say a thing, just lifts a finger and motions for the bartender to bring another. He does. Quickly. I tell him to leave the bottle. After a nod from my brother, he does and then scurries away.

We sit in silence for a few very long minutes before either one of us says anything. He finally breaks and starts the conversation. "You want to talk about it?"

"Not really." I drain my second glass of whiskey and grab the bottle to pour myself another.

"So, am I just supposed to sit here and watch you get fucked up? Because, really, I've got a few more important things I could be doing right now."

I turn my head and stare at him, my insides turning black with anger. "Can you just sit here with me and be my goddamn brother? If I want to get my feelings out, I'll call a fucking counselor."

He stares right back at me, reaches for the bottle to pour himself another drink, and shifts back on his stool, his gaze never leaving mine. "I'll sit here all damn night if you need me to, Ben, but I can't read your mind."

"She said I'm damaged goods," I spit out and turn my head to break our eye contact, heat flaring in my cheeks.

"What?" His glass slams down on the bar, and I hear liquid slosh out and land on the bar. "She fucking said that to you?"

I swallow my embarrassment and turn my attention back to him. "Not directly."

"Wait, what?" His brow creases as his head cocks to one side.

"I overheard some of her staff talking. They apparently are under orders to make sure I'm kept clear of Ms. Baldwin and mentioned it was because I'm damaged goods." My brows raise matter-of-factly as I finish explaining.

He's speechless for several long minutes before finally blowing out a long breath. "I don't know what to say to that."

"I do." I take a swig from my glass and slam it down. The warm liquid is starting to turn the black edges of my brain to gray and I like it. "Fuck her."

"Don't you think you should talk to her?"

I watch as he uses a napkin to wipe up the whiskey he spilled a moment ago. "What the fuck for? More insults? More fake smiles? No thanks." I shake my head and let more of the warm liquid slide down my throat.

"Ben, you know how gossip is. Shit gets misconstrued, made up, twisted, and honestly, this doesn't sound like the Jill I met. I don't take her for someone to dismiss another over a disability, let alone speak about it to others."

I shrug. I'm tired of talking about this shit. "Whatever. I've been calling her for days. She's obviously made her choice."

"So, now what?"

"What do you mean?" I glance over at him.

"What's your plan? Are we ditching the Serenity deal?"

Ah, I knew business was going to play into this sooner or later. It always does with my type A, controlling as hell brother. I scoff. "My plan is to sit here and get fucked up. Then maybe I'll pick up the first gorgeous woman I see, bring her up to a suite, and fuck Jill out of my system."

I grin wickedly at him, pretending that's all I would actually need to forget a woman like Jill, that I even want to be with another woman, and then continue. "You want Serenity still; it's all yours. But I'm out."

"I could give two shits about the deal, Ben. It's not like we need the goddamn money. If you're out, I'm out." He takes a sip of his drink and keeps talking. "But instead of wasting away here, why don't you head out to my place in the Hamptons? It's empty, and its quiet. You can do whatever the hell you need to for a few days."

I cock my head in his direction and consider his suggestion. Getting out of this city, away from my loft that still carries her lingering scent, to stare at the shore for a few days while I shake her out of my system actually seems like a good idea. "Okay."

"Really?" He's surprised and I don't blame him. I'm not usually this agreeable.

"Sure. What the fuck else have I got to do?" I take another drink and then say quietly, "My bed is haunted with her scent. I'm not ready to deal with that yet."

His hand reaches out and clasps around my arm in a tight, knowing grip. "Let me get David to drive you. He's got my car outside and waiting for me anyway. I'll take a cab home."

"Right now?" I question in surprise.

"Bring the damn bottle with you if you need to, Benny. Let's just get you the hell out of here."

I roll over on the couch, my arm smacking into the empty whiskey bottle sitting on the nearby coffee table, sending it crashing to the floor. I sit up, grabbing my forehead as I do, and listen. Did I just hear the doorbell ring? I stand, my leg stiff as fucking hell from being in the prosthetic all night, and glance out the window. It's pouring and the sky is a dark, turbulent gray, which matches my mood perfectly.

I turn my head abruptly again when I hear loud

knocking against the door. Okay, so it wasn't my imagination. But then, who the hell would be crazy enough to come out here in the middle of a fucking raging storm? I stride to the door and yank it open, not bothering to look through the peephole first, and my mouth falls open.

Standing before me, looking like a drowned rat, is a shivering Jill. I stare at her for a long moment, trying to decide if I want to slam the door in her face, but of course, I can't. No matter how pissed off and hurt I am over what she said, I'm not a fucking asshole, and I'm not going to leave her standing in the freezing rain.

I step to the side and motion for her to come in. "What the hell are you doing here?"

Jill-24 hours earlier...

The knock on my office door startles me. Every time someone knocks, I am afraid that Ben will be on the other side of it. Or maybe I am secretly hoping that it will be him. I'm such a damn mess.

"Yes?" I call out.

The door opens, and Aisha peeks her head around the corner. "Hey, Jill, you got a minute?"

I smile. Relieved or disappointed, I'm still not certain. "Sure, come in."

Aisha steps into my office, closely followed by Anna. The two of them stand before me as if they are students in front of the principal. I raise a brow. "Did something break?"

They share a look, one that I don't like.

"Okay, what broke?"

"Nothing broke," Anna mutters. "But we did kind of mess up."

I frown. "Sorry, ladies, I'm very busy, so can you please spit it out?" My voice is laced with irritation I can't hide.

They share yet another look. "We were talking in the hall, and we think—no, we *know* that he heard us."

"What in the world are you talking about?" My brow creases in confusion.

Another shared look.

"Will the two of you stop doing that?" I bark.

Anna bites her lip. "We were talking about you and Mr. Sapphire… And, well, we may have been joking a little bit and he overheard us," Aisha says.

My stomach drops.

"I swear, we didn't know he was there," Anna defends.

My nostrils flare as I press my lips in a firm line. I close my eyes for a moment, pinching the bridge of my nose in an attempt to reign in my temper. "Where is Mr. Sapphire now? And don't you dare share another damn look."

"He left."

"He left?"

"And what exactly was said that upset him so?"

Both of their faces scrunch up, and I already know that I am *not* going to like what they have to say. "Well, I was telling Aisha that I overheard you tell Maria that she was to deal with Ben—um, I mean, Mr. Sapphire—and she asked me why. So, I told her that you said you were tired of damaged goods."

I'm stunned silent for a moment while I absorb what this means. *He thinks that I called him damaged goods? Oh my God.*

"The fact that you two know better than to talk trash in my place of business is one thing, but to gossip so openly about someone I'm dating is completely unprofessional. I promise you two right now, that I will not tolerate this if it happens again."

Aisha and Anna nod.

"Not that it is any of your business, but you were grossly mistaken. What I actually told Maria is that Ben is too good to be dealing with damaged goods. *Me* being said damaged goods."

Anna bites her lip, and I see tears glistening in her eyes. "We are really sorry. We promise, we won't ever do anything like this again."

Imagining how he must have felt when he heard them talk like that makes me sick to my stomach. "See to it that it doesn't. I wasn't kidding. Anything like this again and I will not hesitate to fire you on the spot."

Their eyes widen.

"Understood?"

They nod in unison.

I wave at the door, making it clear they should leave, which they do, fast and with their tails between their legs.

I pick up my cell and scroll quickly to his number. It rings and rings and rings. Fuck. No answer. I punch in a text, and seconds later, Raeva responds, informing me that she is on her way with a car.

I try Ben again, but this time it doesn't even ring; it goes straight to voicemail. Argh!

I grab my keys and my purse and head to the front of the building so that I won't waste any more time than I need to.

I pace the pavement in front of Serenity, stewing, a mixture of anger and anguish flowing over me in waves. A town car pulls over just ten minutes after I text Raeva, and I recognize it to be one of the Kingsley vehicles. Raeva's driver-slash-security guard, Simon, gets out and opens the door for me. I smile at him and thank him as I slide into the car next to her.

"What is the emergency? Where are we headed?" she asks.

"Ben's place."

She raises her brow but provides Simon with Ben's address.

"Now, what the hell is going on?"

I am still shaking with anger when I tell her everything Aisha and Anna told me.

"Shit," she says when I am done talking.

"I know."

Raeva leans in and instructs Simon to step on it. "Yes, ma'am."

We pull in front of Ben's place just minutes later, and I practically fly out of the car before we have even come to a full stop. "Wait for me, please," I yell over my shoulder.

I run up to the elevator across from the gym and press the button. I wait a beat and press again. Damn it. I pull my cell from my pocket and try to dial his number again, knowing that he won't answer, but still, I try.

I sigh as I slide the phone back into my pocket. I turn around and see that the gym is open. Maybe he's there? I stride over to the gym entrance and walk to the front desk. A pretty redhead is on the phone, giving someone a piece of her mind. My first thought is that *I like this girl*. She's feisty. She smiles and holds up a finger before finishing up the call.

"Hi, my name is Stacy. Welcome to Baker-Landon-Rose Memorial Gym. How can I help you today?"

I flash a shy smile at her. "Hi, I'm Jill. I am actually looking for Ben."

She looks me over. "Hmmm, so you're Jill, huh?" she says with a smirk. "I've got to hand it to him; he's got excellent taste."

I feel my cheeks heat, and I'm not sure if it's the compliment, the fact that she clearly has heard about me, or both.

"Oh, and humble, too. Score," she jokes.

I nod, not quite knowing what to say.

"I'm sorry, Ben isn't here. He called earlier to say that he was going to be away for a few days. I actually assumed he was going to be out of town with you."

I'm not sure why that surprises me. But, also, now I am stuck. How am I going to find him? I thank Stacy for her time and make my way back to the car. Simon sees me coming and comes around to open the door. I slide next to Rae feeling defeated. I let out an audible sigh of frustration.

"Not home?" she guesses.

"Nope, and not at the gym either. The girl at the front desk told me that he is going to be out of town for a bit."

I drop my head backwards. "What am I going to do now? I can't bear the thought of him thinking that I would ever say something like that about him."

We drive home in silence, and when we get to the penthouse, I am not in the mood to talk to anyone. I kick off my shoes and crawl into bed, not even bothering to take off my clothes. I wrap myself in the duvet like a little caterpillar in a cocoon.

I try to call Ben once more, but it goes straight to voice-mail again. So, I punch in a text, asking him to please call me. I sigh and bury my face in the pillow. And I don't emerge till morning...

Loud knocking on my bedroom door has me sitting straight up.

"Wake up, sleepyhead."

I groan. "What do you want, Rae?"

"Open the door, Jillybean. We have a phone call to make."

I walk to the door to flip the lock then crawl back into the bed.

"Really? You didn't even bother undressing?" Rae says as she wrinkles her nose.

"Are you here just to lecture me, Mom?" I say a little more irritated than I intended.

"Testy this morning, are we?" She tosses back at me, unaffected by my mood.

'I'm sorry, Rae. I'm just feeling like crap. I still haven't been able to reach Ben and I haven't heard back from him. I don't know what to do."

"Well, lucky for you, your person is brilliant," she says with a triumphant smirk.

I raise a brow. "That a fact?"

"Yup."

"And what brilliant idea do you have, pray tell?"

"I know how to find Ben…"

I sit up, my full, undivided attention on her. "How?" I say eagerly.

"We call Hannah." She cocks her head, grinning from ear to ear.

Hannah is awesome, even though she makes it abundantly clear how upset she is that Ben is hurt. She listens to my side of the story; seeming relieved that there was a reasonable explanation for what happened.

We are not particularly close, but I have always liked her. She tells me where to find him and makes me promise to make it better. I promise that I will try. She clearly loves her brother-in-law dearly.

I ask Raeva if I can borrow the faster-than-lightening car she received for her birthday so I can make it to Drew and Hannah's place as quickly as possible. She hands me the keys without hesitation, and smiling gratefully, I hug my bestie and thank her.

"Go get your man."

The drive seems to take forever. It takes just a little under two hours from Manhattan to the Hamptons, and that's when there's no traffic. I am impatient to see him. And, let's be honest, patience isn't one of my strong points. I make good time, though. My mind is racing the entire time. There are dark clouds in the distance and I wonder if it's a sign of things to come.

The GPS tells me that I'm ten minutes out, which pulls me out of my thoughts and back to reality. It's only now I notice my knee is bouncing like its doing a jig. I feel restless and rake a hand through my hair. I've been gripping the steering wheel so tightly that my hands actually hurt. And, like the bad omen I was afraid of, the sky opens up and rain starts to pour down as if the heavens are flooding.

Just perfect.

I am grateful when I pull up and see lights on in the house. I park in the driveway and sit in the car for a few minutes, just staring at the front door. I try to control my rapid breathing and calm the nerves that have crept up from deep within. I finally get out of the car to brave the pouring rain. Trying to minimize the damage, I run as fast as I can, but by the time I reach the front door and use the knocker, I am soaked from head to toe.

After pounding a second time and becoming even more drenched, the door swings open and I actually flinch in surprise at his disheveled appearance. I realize instantly that no amount of preparation would have helped to control the array of mixed feelings swirling through me at this very moment. The hurt in his expression, and the unfamiliar flash of anger that mars those always sparkling eyes of his, is almost too much to bear.

"Hi," I whisper through trembling lips.

He steps aside and motions for me to come in. "What the hell are you doing here?"

"I had to see you. I had to explain."

"There really is no need. I think I get it."

I sigh. "Ben, you really don't understand. I—"

He puts a hand up to stop me. "I'm missing a leg Jill, but there is not a damn thing wrong with my hearing."

"Damn it, Ben!" I plead with force. "Will you just shut up for one second and let me talk?"

He raises a brow but gestures for me to continue.

"First, I should have called you back to thank you for the flowers and to explain why I stopped returning your calls. Please believe me when I tell you it had nothing to do with you."

I pause, hesitant to admit my truth, but knowing I need to in order to be fair to him. "This is all about me and my fear of letting people in. I swear." I take a step closer to him and fix my gaze on his. "What you heard those two women say; it was them repeating something I said but they got the context completely wrong."

I shiver, some of it from the wet clothes I'm standing it, but also because his stare is cold and unrelenting. He doesn't say a word, so I continue. "Yes, I told Maria to deal with you regarding business because I knew I needed to put some distance between us. But, I told her it was because you've had enough damaged goods in your life and didn't need more." I point to myself. "I'm the damaged goods here,

Ben. Not you. My heart just doesn't work like everyone else's."

My voice becomes shaky as I try and control the emotions now beginning to seep into my tone. "I know that I pushed you away, but it most definitely had nothing to do with you. And yes, you may be missing a part of your leg, Ben, but there is not a damn thing wrong with you. I don't give a fuck about your leg. You are more of a man than anyone I have ever encountered."

He's silent for a moment and then speaks matter-of-factly. "You shouldn't have driven here in this weather. What were you thinking?"

An exasperated chuckle leaves me. "I had to see you. I had to try to explain. The thought of you thinking you were less than whole; I couldn't live with that. I tried calling, but you wouldn't answer. So, here I am." I shrug my shoulders.

"Yes, speaking of that. How *did* you find me?" He scratches his beard, still watching me.

"Hannah," I admit. "But don't be mad at her. She ripped me a new one before hearing my side."

He seems to relax, because he smiles for the first time since I arrived. "She can be a giant pain in my backside, but I love her," he confesses with affection in his voice.

Our gazes meet, and we gravitate to one another like magnets. But then, he stills, taking a step back. "We should get you out of those wet clothes. I'm sure Hannah has something that will fit, and you can use the shower in the guest room." He motions to the stairway. "It's the second door on the right up there. I'll leave some clothes on the bed for you."

I'm not sure what I was expecting, but I feel a twinge of disappointment. I know I have no right, since I'm the one who ruined any chance of us being together. So, I plaster a smile on my face and thank him before heading to the room he directed me to.

I take a quick shower and dry my hair, and when I emerge from the bathroom, I find a pair of jeans and a sweater laying on the bed. Thoughtfully, he also miraculously provided underwear that still has the tags on them. My bra is still soaked so I forgo wearing one. Once I am dressed, I go on the hunt for Ben and find him in the kitchen, making sandwiches.

"Hey there," I say, a bit shyly.

"Hey there, yourself." He favors me with a small smile, those dimples I love so much appearing. "I made some coffee, and I thought I'd feed us."

Ben hands me a plate with a baguette, which I gratefully accept. I didn't realize how hungry I was until I smelled the food. We head to the breakfast nook and sit. I want to tell him that I was wrong, that I've missed him, and that I want us to try to work things out. But before I have a chance to open my mouth, he starts speaking.

"I'm glad you came to straighten things out."

I smile at him, a glimmer of hope spearing through my heart.

"I had some time to think before you showed up." He drums his fingers on the counter for a brief second, glancing down at them as he continues talking. "I realized that perhaps you were correct all along and we should have kept things strictly professional from the start. I want you to know that what happened with you was special to me, but I understand if it wasn't for you, and that I'll let it go and move on."

I feel like he just punched me in the gut. As quickly as my appetite appeared, it disappears. I take a bite anyway, because I am not sure that I can keep my voice from breaking if I speak. So, instead, I chew and nod my head, averting my eyes from his.

"If you are still interested, we should push ahead with our deal. I don't want what happened to affect your willingness to work with us."

Forcing a smile, I take another bite and nod. "Thank you," I tell him with the most even tone I can muster up.

What the hell is wrong with me? This is what I told myself I wanted, so why does my heart feel like it just fell out of my chest. All I know is I deserve this, that I was right all along. I knew this would end in heart break, only the culprit wasn't Ben. It was me.

By the time we finish eating, the weather seems to have improved, so I inform him that I need to be headed back to the city. I thank him for hearing me out and offer work as my excuse to leave. He doesn't argue. We hug as we say goodbye, and I inhale his scent one more time before I whisper goodbye and practically stumble to the car and drive away.

Be careful what you wish for I guess.

As Jill leaves, I close the door behind her and lean my head against the door jamb, fighting an internal battle about whether to chase her or let her go.

For once, reason prevails, but it doesn't stop me from shoving off the frame to move to the closest window and watch as she slides into the sleek car she arrived in. It's several minutes before the engine come to life, and I wonder if she's feeling as much regret as me. The car pulls out of the long drive, but I don't look away until I can no longer see the red taillights through the mist.

I hope I didn't just make the biggest fucking mistake of my life. I believe every word that fell from her sad pink lips, and I also know without a shadow of a doubt that she feels as much for me as I do for her. But I also know, especially after feeling the darkness begin to creep into my soul yesterday, that I absolutely can't let that happen again.

Opening myself up to her, even just the small fraction I'd allowed so far, had made me far more vulnerable than I wanted to be.

I stand at the window, staring at the rain pouring down, until my stump begins to throb in complaint. I've had the damn prosthetic on for way too long and my body has had enough. I tear myself away and decide a visit to the hot tub is in order. Drew was smart enough to build an enclosure around the tub so that it could be used year-round, and I could kiss him right now for his brilliance.

No one is here, so I decide to live on the wild side and strip naked instead of finding a suit. I remove my leg when I reach the edge of the tub, then slide my body down into the steaming hot water with a sigh of relief.

As hard as I try not to let my thoughts wander to Jill, it's the only place my mind seems to want to go. I know, even in the short time we spent together, that she could have been the one and it's the first time I'm allowing myself to admit it. Now that she's gone, of course. I chuff out loud as I think of the old cliché, 'you'll know when the right person comes along' and feel pissed that it's actually fucking true.

"So, why'd you let her go, asshole?" I say it out loud, even though I know there's no one around to hear it, but maybe to make sure I realize I may have just fucked up royally. I'm a coward for pushing her away instead of putting myself in the line of fire again, but damn it, the thought of any more loss in my life is more than I think I could bear right now. No, I made the right decision. I just need to learn to live with it. I'll find other women to spend my time with; that has never been a problem for me. I blow out a long breath, lean my head back, and force myself to push her out of my conscience.

I've been back in the city for the last two days and know a visit to Drew and Hannah's is overdue, so I find myself leaving my loft and walking one block down to their place. Yeah, it's convenient having them so close, and nice. Knowing I have loving people only a few doorsteps away provides a comfort to me that I truly cherish.

I make my way through the lobby and into the elevator, the doorman nodding a friendly greeting at me as I pass. I punch the button for their place, wait until the doors slide open again when the elevator reaches their apartment.

They own the two top floors of the building. But, I mean, hey, they already have two kids and it wouldn't surprise me if they popped out a few more, so the space definitely seems to be a requirement for them. I knock on the door and wait for someone to answer.

The door swings open a minute later, and seeing no one at eye level, I shift my gaze lower to find my spunky little niece smiling up at me. "Uncle Benny!" She doesn't hesitate to run and hop up into my arms, her little hands wrapping around my neck to hug me tight.

She lets go after a moment and scrunches her face up at me, one little finger moving to point at me in a scolding motion. "Where have you been, Uncle Benny? You haven't come to see me in over a week!"

I lean over and pretend to bite her finger, which causes her to screech and clutch onto me tighter as giggles ensue. I place a few kisses on the top of her curly blonde locks and then give her my most practiced puppy dog look. "Sorry, Gracie. I went out of town for a few days."

Her head bobs up and down in understanding. "Uh-huh. Mommy said you were getting your head screwed back on." She leans over, cupping her small hand around my ear, and whispers into it. "But I don't think I was supposed to hear that."

One side of my mouth cocks up into a half-smile as I whisper back, "That can be our little secret then, okay?" Her head bobs up in down in silent agreement, her brown eyes wide with relief. "Where are Mommy and Daddy?"

Grace is actually Hannah's child with her first husband, my friend Jackson, who I served alongside with overseas. He was killed in action shortly after I lost my leg, and unfortunately, never got to raise this beautiful baby girl.

Drew married Hannah a little over a year ago and, shortly after, adopted Gracie as his own. As I look down at her adoringly, I think she may be the most beautiful creature on this planet, except for Jill of course.

I stop in my steps as I realize she's managed to creep back into my thoughts and silently curse myself.

"Whattsa matter, Uncle Benny?" *How are kids so damn intuitive?*

I plop another kiss down on her head and smile at her. "Not a thing, funny face. So, where's Mommy and Daddy?"

"Mommy is giving Brody a bath 'cause he pooped all over himself. It was so gross! You should have seen it, Uncle Benny. I thought Mommy was going to barf!" She throws a hand over her mouth to try to contain her giggles.

"I think I'm glad I didn't, thank you very much!" I ruffle her hair and head toward the kitchen area. "And Daddy?"

"He's not home yet." Her mouth turns down in a little frown. She's got my brother wrapped around her little finger, and I'm sure that when he is home, she's probably got him playing dolls, or having tea parties, or whatever it is six-year-old girls do.

"Well, I guess it's a very good thing I came over then, isn't it?" I sit her down on the kitchen island and slide onto the stool next to her. I glance at my watch to check the time and then back at her. "Have you had dinner yet?"

"Nope." Her blond curls fly back and forth with each shake of her head. "Mommy said after Brody's bath."

"Well, why don't I make you something then? Grilled cheese sound okay?" I stand and wait for her response.

"Yes!" She claps her hands gleefully and bounces on the counter. "Can I help, Uncle Benny?"

I lower myself so that my face is even with hers and speak softly. "Yes, but only if you stop calling me Uncle Benny and just call me Uncle Ben."

Her brows furrow as her eyes squint in thought. Her tiny hands reach out, and she places one of each side of my stubbly cheeks, holding my face in place before speaking to me in a most serious tone. "But Daddy said you love being called Uncle Benny."

I laugh heartily, causing her to jump in surprise, a look

of confusion on her face. "Your daddy is a troublemaker, that's what he is, Gracie!"

She frowns as if this can't possibly be the case and then turns her head and smiles brightly as her mother enters the room. "Who's a troublemaker?"

"Uncle Benny said Daddy is! Does that mean he's in trouble, Mommy?" Her eyes shoot back and forth between Hannah and I, waiting for an answer.

Hannah's brow arches high as she shakes her head. "If Uncle Benny isn't careful, he's the one that's going to be in trouble."

I laugh out loud and then walk over and kiss her on the cheek in greeting. "Hey, Hannah." She gives me a quick hug and a gentle smile as she returns my greeting. "I was just going to make the doodlebug here a grilled cheese."

Her eyes open wide and turn toward her daughter. "Grace Rose Sapphire, you had a grilled cheese for lunch and for dinner last night, too. You're going to turn into a grilled cheese sandwich if you aren't careful."

"But, Mommy, I like them." She lifts her shoulders and blinks rapidly like this should be the most obvious thing ever and not a problem at all.

Hannah walks over, pecks a kiss on Grace's nose, and then lowers her to the floor. "I'll make you dinner. Go play for a little bit and I'll let you know when it's ready."

"Okay, Mommy." She smiles and waves at us both before skipping out of the room.

Hannah turns to look at me and offers me a sympathetic smile. "You doing okay?"

I nod. "Yeah, yeah, I'm good." I pace around her to sit

back on the stool I occupied earlier. "Thank you, by the way."

She tilts her head, one brow raised in question. "For?"

"Cleaning my loft. Changing the sheets." I look down and fidget with a fork sitting on the counter. "I appreciated coming home to…" I look up at her again and shrug. "Well, you know."

Her hand falls over mine and squeezes gently. "We're family, Ben. We do what we can for each other, even if it doesn't seem like very much at all."

I look up into her soft caramel eyes and smile warmly. "My brother sure got lucky when he found you."

She shakes her head and laughs. "Well, technically, he won me in an auction, but that's another story."

I chuckle. "Do you happen to know if there's another one like you I could maybe look into buying?"

Her eyes darken and her smile disappears. "I think, Ben, that you may have already found what you're looking for. Maybe you just need to give it another chance?"

"Hannah, I love you, but I don't want to go there right now, okay? I came over here to try to get her off my mind. So, let's just drop it, okay?"

She sighs. "Fine, but I just want to say one thing."

I look at her, exasperation in my voice. "Do I have a choice here?"

"Not really." She shrugs like I just need to deal with it. "I just want you to know that I was at the spa the other day and saw Jill. She looked miserable, maybe even sadder than you."

"Hannah—" I try to interrupt her, but she slaps her hand over my mouth to shut me up.

"Quiet. I'm almost done." I nod and she removes her hand. "All I was going to say is that it doesn't make sense to me that two people who are so miserable apart should stay that way when they so obviously don't want to be."

I stare at her, my expression blank, and wait to see if she has anything else to add. If she slaps her hand over my mouth again, I may snap. When she remains quiet, I speak. "You done?"

She nods her head contritely.

"It's over." I move to stand in front of her and speak more quietly. "And I'm fine, okay? Or, I will be, so just drop it."

Her eyes shift to the floor, but she nods her head in acceptance. I change the subject quickly, trying to turn the mood in a better direction. "So, where's my baby brother anyway?"

"Work. Closing some deal." She looks at me and lifts her shoulders. "I didn't ask for details. But, hey, what are you doing this Friday? Want to come to dinner with us? There's a fabulous new restaurant that we got reservations for. It's called Indigenous. Have you heard of it?"

I shake my head. "Nope."

"Well, it's getting amazing reviews, and anyone who is anyone has been going, so I got Drew to snag us a table. What do you say?"

I shrug. "Sure. I'm always up for a good meal. Sounds good."

"Awesome!" She claps her hands in delight at my acceptance and I smile. Sometimes, it's the simplest things that make women happy. "Now, are you going to make those grilled cheeses? Because I'm sick of cooking them!"

I spend the next hour cooking, eating, and laughing with Hannah and Grace. She put Brody to bed after his bath, so I missed him but knew I'd see him soon. I leave around eight so Hannah can put Grace to bed, promising I'd see her again on Friday for dinner.

It has been seven excruciating days since I drove to the Hamptons to see Ben. Seven days since I left my heart laying on the floor of that kitchen. Seven days I've been burying myself so deep in work that I have barely seen anyone.

Even at work, I stay in my office. I get there before we open, and I leave long after we close. When the cleaning crew comes in, I've been sending them home and scrubbing the place from top to bottom myself. Anything to keep busy and people out of my hair. I haven't even done a single treatment this week. I just can't be around anyone right now.

Aisha and Anna have been picking up the slack without a single complaint, probably because they still feel bad about what happened the last time Ben was here. I still cringe when I think about it.

It's even worse when I remember the look on Ben's face when he opened the door for me in the Hamptons.

How gutted he looked. All I wanted was to take that pain away.

I shake my head. I need to stop thinking about him. I need to stop missing him. I need to accept that it is over. My phone buzzes on my desk and I glance at it. It's Raeva, and I know what she wants. Mikaela and Rae have been worried about me, and have been relentless with the well-meaning nagging.

I let it ring. But it doesn't take long for me to realize how naïve I was for thinking she would let that slide. Rae is tenacious when she has her mind set on something. Raeva and Mik storm into my office without knocking, armed with boxes of Chinese food and wine.

I glance at them and arch a brow. "Come in, please. Make yourselves at home." Sarcasm drips from every word.

Neither of them seem bothered..

"I called, but since you didn't answer, here we are." Rae shoots back. She places the take-out boxes and some chop sticks in front of me. "Now eat."

I know better than to argue with her when she uses that tone of voice. It's her stern nurse voice, and let me tell you, she knows how to use it. I open a box and shovel some noodles into my mouth. I'm sure they are amazing, but I don't even taste them.

Mikaela fishes a corkscrew out of her bag and opens the bottle of wine. My two besties sit on the chairs across from me, and for a while, we eat in silence.

"Do you remember my new friend Mackenzie?" Mikaela asks me.

I nod. "The chef?"

"That's the one," Mik says with a smile.

"Well," Rae continues. "We are planning a little dinner tomorrow night for River, to celebrate the new software program he designed. And we are having it at Indigenous—Mackenzie's place."

"I really am too busy, but thanks for the invite."

"Oh, please. Too busy doing what?" Mikaela rolls her eyes. "Wallowing in your own self-pity?"

"I'm not wallowing. I am trying to run a business." I retort.

"A business that will run just fine without you while you go out for dinner, particularly because you close around that time anyway."

I realize how lame my excuse is the second it rolls out of my mouth. Leave it to my friends to call me out.

"River really wants you to come. You know he adores you and hates our dinner parties. He says it'll be bearable with you there."

I groan. Of course, she is playing the guilt trip ploy. The last thing I want is to go out in public and entertain people. But, River has always been like a little brother to me; the two of us are thick as thieves. He is brilliant, dresses quirky, and makes me laugh. Maybe, hanging out with River for a night is just what the doctor ordered. Rae and Mik stare at me expectantly.

"Okay," I concede. "I'll go."

"Good," Raeva states smugly.

"I'm picking you up from work at 5:00 pm sharp. I have dresses for us, and we need time to get ready," Mik informs me with excitement.

She gets a little zealous about clothing, and she should; her designs are amazing. Mikaela Kingsley is a fashion queen. Clothing, interior, she does it all. In fact, she did the design for her friend's restaurant. I've not seen it yet, but I'm excited to see her work.

I know picking me up and dressing me is a guarantee to make sure I don't cancel last minute, and I appreciate the gesture. I muster up a smile.

"Okay. I'll be ready."

"Good girl," Rae says as she refills my cup. "You've earned some more wine."

Mikaela smirks at Rae's joke, and I roll my eyes. When I look at my friends and see how much effort they are putting into making sure I am okay, it fills me with warmth.

"Hey, guys?"

"Yeah?" they say in unison.

"Thank you."

"What's family for?" Rae tells me.

"Cheers to that!" Mik chimes in.

I take the elevator from my loft down to the lobby and walk into the brisk night air to wait for Drew and Hannah. They texted a moment ago and told me they were on their way.

I glance at my reflection in the glass window from the lobby and note that what I've worn definitely reflects my mood. I'm dressed completely in black. Black Prada suit, black dress shirt, and black shiny shoes. *All the better to go with my black heart.* I shake my head in defeat over how I feel as of late.

Before I can mull over it any further, a sleek black—*how fitting*— Escalade pulls up to the curb, the window lowering to reveal Drew, a smirk on his face. "Looking for a date?"

I walk to the vehicle, open the door, and step inside to sit across from Drew. "If I was, you certainly wouldn't be my first choice."

"No, I don't suppose I would," he drawls back at me, brow raised knowingly.

I shift my gaze to Hannah, who looks radiant, dressed in a striking blue dress, her long blonde hair falling in waves around her shoulders. "You, however, could be." I flash a playful wink at her. "You look stunning."

"So do you!" Her eyes sweep over me quickly. "I like you in black, Ben. Very dark and sexy."

"Uh-um." Drew clears his throat and tilts his head in his wife's direction, brows creased.

She turns her attention to him and smooths a hand down his chest, over his waist, and then rests it on his thigh. "Do you really need me to tell you that I think you're the most gorgeous man to walk this earth, honey?"

One side of his mouth cocks up before he leans over and presses his lips against hers for several seconds. When he pulls away, she lets out a soft breath. "Nope, but I don't want you admiring anyone else either, my love."

While I'm happy my brother is so completely in love, it's difficult not to be irritated. It feels like I came so damn close to having the same thing within reach, but instead of holding tight, I foolishly loosened my grip, any chance of love slipping through my fingers.

"I'd be happy to get another ride if you two would rather be alone." My tone is snarky, but hey, so is my mood.

"Sorry, Ben," Hannah offers, moving her hand from Drew's thigh and placing it in his hand instead. "We'll behave. I promise." She produces a smile that makes it difficult for me to stay grouchy.

We chat about dinner at our parents' the following week,

moving on to what the kids are dressing up as for Halloween, and then we seem to be at the restaurant. We exit the luxury vehicle and move forward to enter the restaurant.

When we walk through the doors, I stop in my tracks, my dick practically getting hard at the decadence before me. The front of the restaurant boasts a whiskey bar unlike any I've seen before, and I know instantly Indigenous just became my favorite restaurant.

I tap Drew on the shoulder and then point to the bar. "I'll meet you at the table. I want to see what they have to offer."

"Ten minutes, Ben." He looks in the direction our table seems to be in. "Don't make me come looking for you."

"Ten minutes." I repeat, confirming his request. I make my way to the bar, pick up the whiskey menu sitting on its surface, and begin browsing. The choices are magnificent, making it difficult for me to decide what to choose, but it also gives me even more reason to come back again.

I finally decide on a glass of Highland Park, the Ice edition, and my mouth waters to taste one of the rarer single-malts to be had. The bartender places the glass in front of me, and I lift it to my lips, pausing when I notice some familiar faces breeze through the door. Mika and Raeva, along with Mikaela stop at the hostess station for only a moment and then carry forward into the restaurant, not noticing my presence. I make a note to stop and say hi to them when I find my table.

I bring the glass to my nose, inhale deeply, and my mouth waters as I take a slow sip, drawing just a small taste into my mouth. I close my eyes to savor the taste but blink my eyes open when I think I hear a familiar voice.

I turn in the direction of the doorway and freeze when I see who it is. Of course, where Raeva and Mik go, Jill is sure to follow. My heart starts to gallop in my chest as I question whether I should go over and say hello or leave her alone, which is very much what I told her I would do.

I stare at her, my eyes raking down her body to admire the very short dress that displays every curve on her perfect body, down her bare thighs and to the black suede knee-high boots she's standing in, making her legs impossibly longer than the already are. *Fuck it.* There's no way I'm not saying hello.

I take my drink in hand and begin to stroll in her direction but pause again when I see the expression on her face change to relief and then joy as a strangely dressed man bursts through the door and waves her purse in the air. "Found it!"

She meets him halfway and throws her arms around him, depositing a kiss to his cheek as she does. "Oh, River, you're my hero! Thank you!"

I'm once again frozen in my tracks, my eyes glued to the scene unfolding before me. I can feel my pulse throbbing in my neck and the flow of my blood roaring in my ears.

Who the fuck is this asshole? And what in the goddamn hell is he wearing? A fucking Hawaiian shirt? Under a suit that I know cost easily over a thousand dollars? This is what Jill is trying to replace me with? And what is he, twenty? He looks like a baby compared to her.

Before I have a chance to respond or move forward, he

sweeps his arm around her shoulders and ushers her into the restaurant. I know my ten minutes is up, and if I don't get my ass to the table, Drew will be on the war path.

Wasting what should have been a savored drink, I raise the glass of Highland Park to my mouth and down it like a shot. I walk forward, slamming the glass on a random table I pass, and enter the dining room to look for Drew and Hannah.

I don't have to go far. And, *Jesus fucking Christ*, can this night get any goddamn worse? As I move closer, I see Hannah instructing a busboy to merge some tables so that we can all eat together as one large party. I scrape my hand down my face, trying to gather some sense of calm, and approach tentatively.

When I'm standing beside Drew, who happens to be looking at me with a 'don't fucking ask me' expression on his face, Jill finally notices my presence, which is made obvious when her mouth falls open, the grip on her date turning white.

"What the fuck, Drew?" I growl under my breath.

He shrugs. "The Kingsleys walked in, we started talking, Hannah invited them to join us, and here we are." He throws a quick glance in Jill's direction and then back at me. "This was obviously *before* Hannah realized Jill was with them."

"I thought this was just going to be a quiet dinner," I growl again.

"Then leave, Ben. No one is forcing you to stay," he snarls right back.

I turn toward him, fire blazing in my eyes. "You think I'm going to leave her here alone with that little fucking prick over there?" I cock my head in Mr. Aloha's direction. "No fucking way."

"Then sit the fuck down and shut up." He walks away to rejoin Hannah, effectively ending our conversation.

"Ben," Hannah calls to me. "Come sit here next to me." She pats the chair beside her, a look of apology in her eyes. I nod and move behind her to slide into the seat she's offered. I lift my head, and my heart stutters when I find a pair of stormy gray eyes staring back at me, as wide with disbelief as mine.

I purse my lips but know I have to be a gentleman, even though my inner caveman is bursting to come out, and force a small smile. "Jill." I nod curtly in greeting.

She offers me a small smile in return and replies, "Ben."

My eyes shift to her right as the man-child she arrived with sits down next to her and drapes an arm across her shoulder. "This okay, Jillybean?"

She nods her head, her eyes darting from him to me, and then back to him again. He's not a complete moron because he obviously notices the tension between us and rises out of his seat to extend his hand to me. "I don't think we've met. River Ray."

I stare at his hand, one I could easily crush in mine, and then lift mine off the table to grasp his. I give it a quick shake and then release it quickly so I don't unintentionally follow through with the dark thoughts running through my mind. "Benjamin Sapphire."

I think I see him falter for a moment as he glances at Jill, but can't be sure, because his movements are as smooth as glass. "I've heard a lot about you, of course. It's nice to finally meet the man in the flesh."

I quirk my eyebrow up, shifting my gaze back and forth between him and Jill and then finally respond. "Unfortunately, I can't claim the same about you. River, you said?" There is no way I'm letting this guy think he's anything but a passing fucking thought in my brain. "What do you do for a living?"

He reaches out, grabs a piece of the fresh bread that was just delivered, butters a slice, and then takes a bite. He shrugs, a smug look on his face as he responds. "A little of this and a little of that."

Without a care in the world over whoever this fucking man-child is, I turn my attention back to Jill and cock my head in a show of disbelief. "Perhaps you should teach him to not talk when his mouth his full. I mean, really, Jill, are you sure he's even old enough to drink?"

Her eyes squint dangerously, and then her red painted lips move to form a sinister smile. "Oh, don't you worry, *Benny*, he more than old enough to drink. In fact, he could probably teach an old dog like you a few new tricks."

"I highly doubt *that* boy could teach me anything." I snort, looking over at her date again, scanning my eyes over his lean frame, and then bring my gaze back to hers. "But if you need a reminder of what I do and don't know, Jill, I'd be more than happy to show you."

I run my thumb over my lip, darting my tongue along its tip as I do, a subtle reminder of just what I can do, and chuckle when I see her cheeks flush pink.

She rises abruptly from her chair, tossing her napkin to

the table, excusing herself before stalking in the direction of the bathroom. Her man-child stands to follow, but I reach across the table and grip his arm in warning. "Stay. I'll go after her. I'm sure I owe her some kind of apology now."

He nods curtly and slides back down into his seat. "Just stop being a dick, man. She deserves better."

I meet his eyes for a moment and nod, knowing he's right, and then stride after Jill. Instead of going to the restroom, though, she walks to the entrance of the restaurant and steps outside. By the time I follow after her, she's walking in long strides back and forth in front of the building.

When I exit, she stops, spins on her heel, and marches up to me, her finger spearing me in the chest as she begins yelling. "Just who the hell do you think you are, Benjamin Sapphire? You have no right. None! How dare you insult my friend like that, and then blatantly come on to me in front of the entire table!"

I open my mouth to speak, but she stabs her finger into my chest again. I know I shouldn't feel this way, but seeing her angry like this only makes me realize how much I want her. She's so goddamn sexy when she's trying to be tough with me. "No! I don't want to hear one word you have to say! I've heard enough out of you!"

"You know what, Jill?" I pluck her tiny hand from my chest, wrap it in mine, then push my body against hers, backing her up until she's forced up against the brick wall of the building. I take her other hand and press it above her head, stepping forward into her body so mine is completely flush with hers, ensuring there's no question about how I feel. "There's not a goddamn thing I want to say to you anyway. But I sure as fuck know what I want to do to you."

Before she can say another word, I slam my mouth against hers in fury. I kiss her until I feel her knees weaken underneath her, and her chest is rising in short pants against mine. I kiss her until I feel her hand grip onto the back of my neck and her fingernails dig into my skin. I kiss her until I finally feel her soften under me, and only then do I let her go.

We both are breathing hard and staring at each other in confusion. "Jesus Christ, Jill. What the fuck are you doing to me?" I rake my hand through my hair and then shake my head in an attempt to clear it. I take a step closer and cup her face in my hand, a feeling of regret washing over me.

"I'm sorry. So fucking sorry." And then I turn and walk away from her, fleeing the restaurant and her as quickly as I can.

Jill - 3 hours ago....

As promised, Mik shows up at five sharp in one of the Kingsley vehicles to pick me up. I am under no illusion that I have any say regarding any of this, so I am ready and waiting for her to arrive.

As soon as I'm home, I'm ordered to my bedroom to take a shower to get prepped. After I dry my hair, I shrug into a robe and head to Mikaela's room, where I also find Rae, both of them in Mik's dressing room.

"Champagne?" Rae asks as she holds a glass out for me.

I gratefully accept. If I am going to be any fun tonight, I need a little buzz.

"Look what I got for you," Mikaela says in a sing song voice.

She holds out a beautiful leather dress that has thousands of little spots in a variety of colors painted atop of it. It almost looks like dragon skin; it's beautiful. I tell her so and she beams.

"Put it on," she says.

I eagerly accept the gorgeous garment and slip it over my head. Raeva helps me zip up while Mikaela stands in front of me, appraising her masterpiece. She claps her hands together and squeals with glee. I think she approves. Her reaction makes me giggle, and I realize that I have just laughed my first genuine laugh in a week. Maybe tonight is exactly what I need.

"Wait!" Rae exclaims. "I have the perfect boots to go with these. Be right back."

She runs off to her own penthouse to get them, leaving me with Mikaela.

"I can't tell you how happy I am to see you smile, Jill."

"I'm not going to lie, it feels good."

I sit at Mik's dressing table, and she positions herself behind me and starts to brush my hair.

"I know how it feels." I look up at her in the mirror. I know that she does, even though she never speaks about it. "And I understand why you walked away."

She searches for my gaze in the mirror and captures it. "I just hope that Ben doesn't turn out to be your Eric, your one and only, because I wouldn't wish this feeling on anyone. Pining for the one man you know you can never have. Knowing that no man will ever understand you the way he does, or who truly see who you are. I love you, and I don't want that for you."

A tear rolls down her cheek. I rise to my feet to pull her into a hug. "Hey," I tell her. "No crying allowed, remember. This is supposed to be a fun night." I pull back enough so that I can wipe the tear from her cheek with the back of my hand and then pull her into another hug.

"Jeez!" Rae exclaims. "Can't I leave the two of you alone for one second?"

Mikaela and I share a look, and she holds her hands up. "My bad." She smiles in apology at Rae. "We're good now."

Raeva nods and then holds up her phone. "River just texted that he's headed this way, so we need to finish getting ready."

Raeva approaches me and whispers in a conspiratorial tone, "I am making him wear a suit."

I scoff. "No way."

"Yeah way."

I laugh. "Now, this, I have to see. Let's finish up, girls!"

When we get downstairs, both Mika and River are standing in the lobby, their backs facing us. The first thing I notice is, not only did River get a haircut, but he is in fact actually wearing a suit. When he turns around, though, I'm pleased to see the River we all know and love is still present.

"River! You promised!" Rae complains with a wrinkled

nose. He holds his hands up in defense. "Hey. I held up my end of the bargain. You said wear a suit. I am wearing a damn suit." He cocks his head, unable to mask the delight on his face. "I even wore the suit you sent over."

I chuckle. Typical rebellious River. He's right, of course; he is wearing a suit—a very nice one at that—only instead of a dress shirt, he has paired it with the loudest Hawaiian-print shirt known to man. I walk over to him and kiss his cheek.

"I, for one, think you look fantastic," I state in support.

River beams at me. "That's because you have excellent taste, my friend."

And, with that, we walk outside and all pile into the silver Lincoln that is waiting at the curb. River blows out a long whistle. "Fancy ride, brother-in-law. New toy?"

"Are you in the market for a new toy, brother-in-law? Because I can set you up with my guy," Mika says with encouragement..

"Boys and their toys," Mikaela says as she rolls her eyes.

Everyone happily chats and jokes during the short ride to Indigenous. When we pull up to the curb, I'm the last one to climb out, River waiting to assist me. We step into the restaurant, and I notice my hands are empty and slap myself on the forehead. "Crap, I left my purse in the car. I'll be right back," I say as I turn to leave.

"Don't be silly, I'll get it." Before I can even respond, he's already shot back outside in search of my purse. I linger at the hostess stand for only a few moments before the door opens, and River steps in waving my purse. I do a little dance as I make my way over to him and throw my arms around him, placing a kiss on his cheek in thanks.

"Oh, River, you're my hero! Thank you!" I beam.

"You're very welcome." River slides his arm around my shoulder to lead me into the restaurant, where we spot our table mates quickly. Only, it seems that we now have a few more guests in our party. Drew and Hannah Sapphire are also here, and the girls are working to have our tables joined for dinner. A bolt of pain flinches through me, followed by relief when I realize Ben doesn't seem to be with them.

I move to greet Hannah and introduce her to River. I ask where Drew is, and she points somewhere behind me. I turn around to wave at Drew, and that's when I see him. The entire planet tilts and falls off its axis, making it feel like the room is spinning out of control. I can feel the color drain from my face as my jaw goes slack. *What the fuck is he doing here?*

My first instinct is to run as my eyes dart to the exit. But, no, I can't let him see that he affects me in any way. I don't want him to think he has power over me, even though I know the truth. *Damnit, he totally does.*

I'm not sure if he's noticed me, but everyone starts to take their seats, and of course, by some damn misfortune, the only two chairs available are directly across from Ben and Hannah. To make matters worse, when River pulls my chair out for me, he reaches for the one directly across from Ben.

What am I supposed to do, act like a child and tell him I don't want sit across from the mean boy that broke my heart? Ugh, that's not even accurate because he doesn't even know he broke my heart. I plaster a smile on my face, thank River, and then gracefully sink into the chair.

I can't help myself, and fix my eyes on Ben to gauge his reaction. I can't believe my heart is betraying me like this; beating out of control, as if she is trying to escape from my chest and jump into Ben's arms.

He looks up and our eyes finally connect. The look on his face speaks volumes; he doesn't want to see me at all. And fuck me if that doesn't hurt like hell, especially after the curt greeting he gives me.

River sits next to me and puts his arm around my shoulder. He knows I always get cold in restaurants. He gestures up, and my eyes follow, noticing the vent blowing cold air above our heads. I see now why he chose this seat for me. He's the one directly under the vent. "This okay, Jillybean?"

I nod my head. I seem unable to keep my eyes from wandering back to Ben. It's as if he is silently calling to me. Or am I making this shit up in my head? I'm not sure what Rae has told River about Ben, but I do know that River can scope out a situation like no other. He introduces himself to Ben, and I get a real strange vibe from the interaction.

There is definitely some kind of silent pissing match happening between them, with me being the object of their attention, which is a ridiculous thought. Ben is the one who stated he wanted to keep things professional between us. Ben looks at me and cocks his head, a look of contempt marring his chiseled features.

"Perhaps you should teach him to chew with his mouth

closed and not talk when his mouth his full. I mean, really, Jill, are you sure he's even old enough to drink?"

Are you fucking kidding me?

I narrow my eyes as my temper tries to get away from me, smiling to disguise my anger. "Oh, don't you worry, *Benny*, he's more than old enough to drink. In fact, he could probably teach an old dog like you a few new tricks."

He scoffs. "I highly doubt that boy could teach me anything." His lip rises in a sneer.

Dick.

"But," he continues, "if you need a reminder of what I do and don't know, Jill, I'd be more than happy to show you."

I can't believe he just said that. I'm so pissed. I sit and stew for a second, watching as he takes his thumb and traces it sexily over his lip, his eyes locked on mine. When he sees me looking, he chuckles. He's such an ass, and I've had enough. I rise to my feet, deposit my napkin on the table, and grab my purse.

"Excuse me, please."

I intend to go to the ladies' room, but I am so angry I know I need more than a moment. When my gaze falls on the exit door, I make a snap decision. "Fuck it," I mutter angrily under my breath.

When I get outside, I realize the car has left. Damn it. I pull out my phone and order a cab. Impatiently pacing on the sidewalk, I wait for my ride when Ben storms out of the restaurant and stands in front of me, forcing me to stop pacing. And I just snap. "Just who the hell do you think you are, Benjamin Sapphire? You have no right. None! How dare you insult my friend like that, and then blatantly come on to me in front of the entire table!"

He opens his mouth, but I don't want to hear a damn thing from him anymore. I am over it. Done. And I tell him so while poking him in the chest.

"You know what, Jill?" he says as he grabs my hand. He towers over me and closes the distance between us. I try to retreat, but not out of fear; I am not scared of Ben. No, I back up out of self-preservation. Because even though this man has just acted like a gigantic ass, my body screams for his.

I want him. Suddenly, there's nowhere else to go. The brick wall that is halting my escape is cold against my back. Ben pushes into me, and I can feel how hard he is. I swallow, raising my eyes to find his blazing ones staring back at me.

"There is not a goddamn thing I want to say to you anyway. But I sure as fuck know what I want to do to you."

The next thing I know, his lips slam against mine and the world falls away. Just when I think my legs are going to collapse under me, he pulls away and looks at me in confusion. Before I can even gather my wits, he's apologizing and then walking away.

I watch in a daze, unable to react. *What the fuck was that?* How could he kiss me like that and then tell me he regrets it? You don't kiss someone like that and regret it. No way. Benjamin Sapphire owes me some answers, and I am going to go get them.

What a fucking mess.

What the fuck did I just do? I tell her we need to keep things professional and then I go and act like a jealous school boy the moment I see her with another man—okay, I still contend he's a child.

My strides are long and heavy as I walk away, afraid to look back, because I'm not sure I'll be able to stop myself from turning around and dragging her back home with me. Why does she have to be so goddamn beautiful, so smart, so irresistibly challenging?

I head closer to the curb so I can hail a cab and am happily surprised, and extremely relieved, when I see the Escalade pull up beside me and the passenger window sliding down. David, Drew's right hand man, is leaning toward the window. "You want me to take you somewhere, Mr. Sapphire?"

I nod and move to open the back door and then settle myself inside the vehicle. "Thanks, appreciate it."

"That's what I'm here for, sir." He pulls smoothly out into traffic and then meets my eyes in the rearview. "Where can I take you?"

I scrub my hand over my rough beard, wondering momentarily if it's time for me to actually shave it, and then shrug. "Home, I guess. I don't think I'm going to be good company for anyone tonight."

"Home it is." Minutes later, we arrive in front of my building, and I help myself out of the back seat and slam the door shut behind me. I give David a short wave of thanks and then turn toward the front doors.

I'm about to go in when my phone starts vibrating against my chest. I reach inside my jacket and pull it out, knowing already it's either going to be Hannah or Drew. I grimace when I see Hannah's name on the screen and swipe left to read her message.

> What in the world is the matter with you? How dare you treat Jill and River the way you did! I'm so mad at you right now, Ben!

I shake my head, knowing I'm going to have to go over and see her tomorrow with my tail between my legs to apologize. Because, of course, she's right. I acted like a complete asshole. My phone buzzes again, and I read the next text from Hannah, a smile small forming on my lips, thinking again how goddamn lucky my brother got.

> David said he took you home. Are you okay? Call me if you need to talk.

I slide my phone back in my jacket pocket and then

enter the lobby of my building, taking the elevator up to my loft. I walk in, shrug my jacket off, and walk straight to the kitchen to pour myself a drink. I think some whiskey is in order, if I do say so myself. Lots and lots of whiskey. Whatever I have to do to get Jill out of my goddamn head.

I grab the first bottle I see out of the cupboard—I have many, mostly gifts from clients and staff—and a glass, then pour myself a good four fingers of the amber liquid. Just smelling it makes my mouth water, and as I take a long pull, I moan in relief.

I head to one of the couches, pulling my shirt from my slacks, working the buttons undone as I go, and am about to sink down when the buzzer for the elevator sounds.

Shit. Maybe Hannah decided she was going to rip me a new one tonight instead of tomorrow. I must have really pissed her off. I stride quickly over to the call button and press the intercom button. "Yep."

"Ben?" I rear back in surprise when Jill's curt voice reaches my ears. She's definitely not who I was expecting.

"Jill?" I respond. "What are you doing here?"

"Let me up, Ben. I have a few things I want to say to you."

Shit. I can hear the anger in her voice and sigh deeply as I press the button to release the elevator. *This should be fucking fun.*

I set my drink down on the table and, moving to stand in front of the elevators, shove my hands in the pockets of my slacks as I wait for her. After what feels like an eternity, the doors slide open, my breath once again catching at her beauty.

She stomps her foot on the floor of the elevator, rolls her eyes, and then storms past me. "Jesus Christ, Ben! Really? Do you have to stand there and look like... like that?" She waves her hand up and down the length of my body.

I look down to scan myself and then back up at her, my brows creased in confusion. "What the hell are you talking about, Jill?"

"Argh!" She slams her purse on the table, twirls around to face me, and places her curled up little fists on her hips. *Jesus, she's fucking adorable when she's pissed.* I can't help the smirk that dances across my lips as I watch her, fascinated.

"You really have no idea, do you?" she spits out. "And wipe that look off your face!"

I watch as she takes a few steps closer to me, her eyes trailing down my bare chest, and then I realize what she meant. Well, fuck, I just scored a point and wasn't even trying. I take a step closer, purposely trying to invade her space, and cheer internally when I see her falter and stand in place.

"Where's your man-child? Won't he be upset that you left him and came running back to me?"

I know I'm pushing my limits here, but if I don't do something to really piss her off, really make her want to leave, I'm going to do something both of us may regret.

"You are such an asshole." She stomps her foot in place again, her hair swishing back and forth as she shakes her head in anger. "First of all, *River* is a friend. He's Rae's younger brother, whom I have known since he *was* a child, so why don't you just put that jealous shit on a shelf and move on!"

My brows raise at the fact that River wasn't her date at all, and I'm immediately torn in two by feelings of relief and then embarrassment for my assumptions and behavior. She must read the emotion on my face because she doesn't wait for me to reply before continuing.

"Yes, not feeling so high and mighty now, are you, Mr. Sapphire?"

I growl and take another step toward her. "Don't call me that. You know I hate it."

She's taunting me now, because she takes a step closer, the distance between us mere inches, and tilts her head up to mine to smile sweetly. "And I hate that you tell me in one breath that we need to keep things professional, but then you act like a jealous beast the first time you see me on another man's arm."

Her breath is coming out in short pants, the heat of it invading my nostrils every time I inhale, reminding me exactly what she tastes like. My gaze flicks to her mouth, her eyes, and then back to her mouth again. The angle of her head changes and rears back slightly, and I know she's registered what I must be thinking.

I want her. I want her so fucking badly that having her this close is making it very goddamn hard not to do what every instinct in my body is screaming at me to do.

I surprise myself, and, I think, her, when I reach forward and cup her face gently in my hands and speak softly. "And that's why I said I was sorry. You deserve better than this, Jill. I'm a fucking mess. You deserve someone whole, and good, and who isn't afraid to love you the way you should be. I'm a broken man, Jill. Maybe beyond repair."

Her eyes crinkle as she scrunches her forehead and looks directly at me as her voice, soothing and sweet, leaves her mouth. "We're all broken, Ben. All of us, in some way. Won't you even try to give us a chance?"

I let my head fall back as I blow out a long breath, my eyes closed as I consider what she's asking me, and then bring my gaze back to hers. "I don't want to hurt you."

Her teeth clench around her bottom lip, her cheeks flushing pink as she looks up at me from under her lashes, and then releases it. Moving herself closer to me, her next words come out in a whisper. "Not being with you hurts more."

That's it. I'm done. It's all I need to hear. I slide my hands behind her head as I pull her body flush to mine and finally, finally, seal my lips against hers. Her hands snake over my chest, against my bare skin, and wrap around my back as she holds on to me. I don't care if this ends with my heart turning to stone. There is nothing I can do to stop the floodgates she's just opened.

This isn't what I came here to do. I came here to give him hell. But, now, all I want is to rip every last article of clothing he's still wearing off his body.

His lips are on mine, his tongue invading my mouth, our breaths becoming one. My entire body is pressed tightly up against him, but it still doesn't seem close enough.

I moan into his mouth, and he responds by grinding up against me, demonstrating just how much he wants me too. Hands are everywhere, as if neither of us can decide where we want to touch first. Ben tears his lips away, panting, his eyes locking with mine as he rests his forehead against me. *Has he changed his mind again?*

I stare back at the stormy blue gaze I always seem to find myself drowning in and am rendered speechless. The virility in his disposition is the sexiest thing I have ever seen.

"If we do this tonight, Jill, no more running. I'll be yours. Every piece of my brokenness will be yours, and you… you'll be mine." He trails his lips from my forehead, slowly moving down until he's peppering my neck with small kisses and little nips. "Every last fucking inch of you will be mine. Is that what you want?" he demands.

I can't find my voice to speak. I'm too mesmerized with him, too consumed with need. So, I just nod. I tremble as his tongue slides across my clavicle. "Say it," he growls. "I need to hear you say the words."

"I do. I want that," I manage to croak.

That seems to be all he needs. In a flash, my dress is pooled around my ankles, and I stand before him in only black lace panties and Rae's knee-high suede boots.

"Jesus Christ, Jill. No bra? Are you trying to kill me?"

I suck my lower lip between my teeth and swing my head back and forth. "It didn't work with the cutouts on the dress." I step demurely out of the material around my feet and push Ben's shirt off his shoulders sending it swishing to the floor.

A mischievous grin appears on my face, and I push against his chest, indicating that I want him against the wall. He cocks his head and raises his brows in delight as he willingly obliges.

Darting my tongue out, I run it quickly over my lips and look up at Ben as I sink to my knees in front of him. I undo his belt, then his button, then grab onto the metal tab of his zipper to slowly pull it down. I tug his slacks down, making sure to take his boxers down as well. His magnificent length springs free and stands in attention in all its glory.

I wet my lips again. I want to taste him so fucking bad. I've not taken my eyes off his once, and I feel an electric spark run through me at the desire in his eyes. I smile, wrap my hands around his cock, and then slide my mouth over its wide crown. I stroke his length with my fingers as my tongue swirls around his head.

I suck, alternating between gentle and a little rough. His hands fist my hair, and he rocks his hips against my mouth. I relax my throat and take him—all of him. I don't take my irises off his when he hits the back of my throat, moaning around him instead, thrilled when I see his head finally fall back, a long groan escaping his lips. The little sounds he makes every time he slides in serves as motivation to keep going, but Ben has different ideas.

He slides out of my mouth, pulls me to my feet, and then hoists me up in the air over his shoulder. I yelp when he smacks my lace-covered bottom and then practically purr at the warm feeling that spreads after. When he reaches the bed, he tosses me onto my back, my body bouncing slightly on its soft surface, a short gasp of excitement leaving me. I like this man-cave act he's displaying.

He sits on the edge of the bed, removes his prosthetic, and then rolls over onto his hands and knee and begins prowling toward me. "My turn," he says with a wicked grin on his face.

He pushes my legs apart and buries his head between them. I can feel his hot breath through my panties, and I let out a soft mewl. His large hands grip either side of my lacy underwear, and in one smooth tug, he yanks at the material, turning it into scraps.

A surprised squeal escapes from me and he chuckles. "I'll buy you new ones," he mutters before diving back down. I forget about the damn panties the second his tongue makes contact with that little bundle of joy he's zeroed in on. He sucks and nibbles and licks long strokes up and down, over and over, driving me to the brink of insanity.

His stroking stops, and I feel the heat of his mouth cover my entire core before he sucks, hard. I surge off the bed, and he shoves me back down with one hand. "Uh-uh, you stay right there, Angel."

His talented tongue keeps playing with my clit as he thrusts two fingers inside of me. "Yes." I nearly come right then and scream out loud.

He plunges his digits in and out of me, changing directions and applying pressure that has me writhing underneath him, all the while continuing his oral pleasure. I can feel my orgasm building in the depths of my belly, and I beg for it, for the sweet relief my body so desperately aches for. "Ben, please," I whimper.

"Please what?" he teases.

"For the love of God, make me come already." I gasp.

He smirks before he takes me in his mouth sucking my clit roughly, and I combust on the spot, screaming his name as I fall over the edge.

I hear the ripping of foil, and before I even have time to come down from my orgasm, he positions himself over my throbbing core and plunges inside of me in one smooth stroke. All of him, every last inch, fills me completely, and I finally feel whole.

He stills for just a moment and then begins to rock against me. It only takes seconds until we're moving in tandem, our bodies slapping slamming into each other. It feels incredible; I don't want this pleasure to ever end. Just as I think those words, he pulls out of me, a loud yelp of protest falling from my lips.

He flashes me that devilish grin of his, then grips my waist, flipping me onto my front. In one second flat, his hands slide to my hips, lift them, and then his cock is thrusting into me from behind. I rock my ass back into his hips, a moan of pure bliss rolling out of me.

One hand snakes across my belly and grasps onto my breast, while the other holds on to my hip, his grip tightening as he begins to piston in and out of me. Long moans fall from my lips as my core starts to tremble once more. I know what's coming and I want it. I want it so, so bad.

"Oh my God," I croak over and over until I explode around him and collapse forward onto my chest, my ass still in the air. He grasps my hips tighter as he starts to chase his own release, pounding into me without mercy. Inwardly, I beg for him to come, while simultaneously praying he'll never stop.

I wake up tightly nested in Ben's strong arms. When I try to move, he clutches tighter.

"Don't you even think about it," he grumbles.

I inwardly swoon, murmuring. "I was just turning around."

He loosens his grip, and I turn to face him, wrapping my arms around him. "Good morning," I mumble with a smile.

He kisses the top of my nose. "Good morning."

"I hate to be all cliché about this, but I have to ask; what now?"

Ben rubs his nose against mine. "I'm not sure what now. All I know is that I am miserable without you."

"I was miserable without you, too," I confess.

"Then let's not be miserable together," he says, grinning.

I giggle, then tease, "Oh, how poetic."

Ben cups my face in his hands and angles my head so that I am staring directly into his eyes. "I wasn't kidding last night, Jill. You're mine now. You chose me, broken and all, and I am not letting you go."

"I need you to hear me when I tell you this, Ben," I plead earnestly. "I am lying here naked in your arms, not just physically naked, but emotionally stripped down. For you. Just for you. You say that you're broken, but dammit, so am

I. But when I am with you… Ben, when I am with you, I feel whole."

A tear rolls down my cheek. Ben leans in and kisses it away. "Well, shit."

I frown. "What?"

"Your speech just blew mine out of the water."

I roll my eyes and playfully slap him on the chest. Ben grabs my hand and brings it to his mouth. "I'm sorry for being a complete asshole last night. Can you forgive me?"

"Can you promise me it will never happen again?"

"I solemnly swear," he says dramatically.

I grin and kiss the tip of his nose. "Then, yes, you're forgiven. But you better apologize to River."

He grumbles but concedes. "I'm glad you came over to rip me a new one," he says with a smirk.

"Stop trying to beat my speech. You won't win," I admonish jokingly.

"Fine," he tells me before flipping me onto my back. "But I bet I can show you a bunch of things I am a champ at."

"Oh? Those sound like fighting words to me," I tell him with a smirk.

"I think I'm up for the challenge," he counters, his gaze turning dark and smoldering.

I look to where his need his pressing firmly against my belly and then back up at him. "I'd say that's more than obvious."

"You better get ready then, Angel, 'cause the games are about to begin."

Now this is the kind of fucked I want to be...

Two glorious months later...

I roll over and smile when my eyes land on the angel taking up residence across half my bed. She's managed to pull almost all of the covers off me and has them wrapped haphazardly over her body, one naked leg curled over the top, seemingly holding all of the blankets prisoner. She starts out at the beginning of the night curled up against me like a kitten, and every morning ends up looking like a caged tiger gone wild.

I move to the side of the bed, fit my prosthetic on, and then rise silently, glancing at the clock. It's still early, just a few minutes after seven in the morning. I smile again because I remember what day it is. It's Christmas, and I couldn't ask for a more perfect gift to wake up to on this day. To have her here in bed every morning when I wake up is still a surprise to me.

But here she is, like she has been almost every single morning since our blow-out at Indigenous back in October. Every single fiber of my being wants to force myself back under the covers and wake her up in a way that will never have her thinking about Christmas morning the same way again, but I don't.

We were up late last night celebrating with Mika, Raeva, and Mikeala, and I know we have another busy day ahead of us today, so I tiptoe out of the enclosed space and head toward the kitchen.

When I reach the room, I press a button to open only the kitchen window shades and stare in wonder when I see the sky outside. Large, fluffy snowflakes are floating down through the air, landing on every available surface to create an enormous blanket of white.

I walk closer to the window to marvel at its simple beauty, my heart filling with joy at everything I have to be thankful for today. I've always thought New York City was beautiful, but witnessing the scene before me leaves me stunned.

Warm hands wrap around my waist from behind, and I sigh as Jill presses her body to mine, resting her head on my shoulder. "Good morning, handsome."

"Merry Christmas, my angel." I turn in her arms and cup her face in my hands, placing a kiss on her lips. "I was trying to let you sleep. I'm sorry if I woke you."

She smiles up at me and leans forward to press her lips against mine. "You didn't. I had to pee." She giggles and then pushes her body against mine in a hug. "And, Merry Christmas to you, too, babe."

I hold her against me, close my eyes, and savor this simple moment. It doesn't last long because she pushes against me and does a little hop-dance move in front of me, her hands clapping together. "Do we finally get to open presents?"

I throw my head back as I laugh out loud and then beam down at her. "How old are you, Jill Baldwin? I don't even think Gracie gets this excited."

"Ben," she drawls out in frustration, "you've been making me stare at wrapped presents under that tree for two weeks. I can't take it anymore!"

I bend down, peck her on the nose, and deliver a slap to her backside that causes her to jump out of reach with a squeal. "Well, Miss Little Impatience, you're going to have to wait ten more minutes because this man needs coffee."

"Ugh." She scampers over to the coffee maker and begins preparing a pot for us, looking over at me while she does, and sticks her tongue out. "Fine, but only because I desperately need a cup, too."

I grab her favorite creamer out of the fridge and place it on the counter near her, dropping a kiss on her head as I pass, and then continue past to pull two mugs out of the cupboard. I hand them to her, and she scoops one sugar and some of the cream in a mug, leaving the other as is. We've developed an easy routine that I, for one, never in my life imagined would happen for me.

"Do you want me to open the rest of the shades, or leave it a little dark so we can enjoy the lights on the tree?"

"Open!" she exclaims with glee. "I want to watch the snow falling. It's so pretty!"

The coffee is almost done brewing, so she fills both mugs before carrying them over and handing one to me. We move in unison to the tree and, without words, both sink to the floor in front of it, looking at the lights twinkling above us, both of us admiring the beauty.

"Ben?" Her voice is soft and quiet as she says my name.

"Yes?"

"This is so beautiful, and it's so romantic, but if you don't let me open a present right this minute, I swear I'm going to scream."

I chuckle and set my coffee on the floor beside me. "Oh, my little Angel, always so anxious." I reach under the tree, pluck out the first gift I have for her, and place it in her eager little fingers.

Her eyes light up, just like a kid on Christmas morning, and she rips into the packaging, tearing it to shreds as she does. She's left with a flat, 8 x 10 box, which she spins around in her hands a few times, shakes, and then finally tears open. She flips the tissue paper open and pulls out the envelope laying inside, her brows creasing in curiosity as she looks up at me.

She lifts the fold and then pulls out the contents, revealing two plane tickets. I wait a minute as she reads the destination, and then grin broadly when she looks up at me, her eyes wide with wonder. "Bora Bora?" She looks back down at the tickets again as if she can't believe they are real, and then back up at me. "You're taking me to Bora Bora?"

I nod enthusiastically, so fucking content that she's happy with my gift. "I overheard you talking with Rae one day about your dream vacation, so..." I shrug and point to the tickets. "Because, baby, I want to make all your dreams come true."

She drops the tickets and lunges herself against me, her arms wrapping tight around my neck as she tackles me. "Thank you, thank you, thank you, Ben!" She pulls her face back enough to press her lips to mine for a few seconds, delivering enough passion to make me want to drag her back to the bedroom, and then leans back to look at me. "You are seriously the most amazing man I could have ever hoped for."

I kiss her now, tugging her back into my arms for another hug. "You deserve this and so many other things I intend to give you, my angel."

When we release each other, I can see she's blinking rapidly, but don't worry because I know it's happiness. I've given this to her, and it fills me with a peace like none I've ever known.

She reaches under the tree to grab a present for me, but I hold up my hand. "Wait, I've got one more for you."

Her mouth falls open and then just as quickly, closes and forms a smile. "I was going to say you should have, but no, if you want to give me more presents today, I'll take them." She's bouncing up and down, her legs under her, and holds out her hands for another offering, her mouth curved into a huge grin.

I laugh and then reach under the tree to pull out a smaller box, wrapped in pretty gold, sparkling paper and place it in her wiggling fingers. Again, no hesitation, just ripping, the paper sitting in shreds on the floor in seconds. She holds it up to her ear, shakes it lightly, and then lowers it into her lap before lifting the cover off the small, square black box.

She gasps when the lid is off, her hand flying to cover her mouth, her wide eyes jumping up to lock onto mine. Her hand slowly lowers from her mouth, and my name rolls quietly from her lips. "Ben…" Her gaze shifts back to the box and then to me again. "This is beautiful."

I reach over, slide the box from her fingers, and run my fingers lightly over the contents. "I had this made just for you." I lift the necklace out of the box, undo the clasp, and then lean forward to secure it around her neck. It's a delicate gold chain, and on the end, her name, Jill, has been spelled out in diamonds. It looks stunning on her.

"The first time I ever laid eyes on you, it was in a dazzling gold dress covered in a million sparkles." I move my gaze from the necklace to look down into her eyes, now even more moist, and offer her a warm smile. "You were the most stunning woman I had ever seen, but you wouldn't tell me your name."

She laughs and nods at the memory. "I remember, Ben. But, to be fair, you were insanely sexy looking and that scared the crap out of me."

I chuckle and grasp her hand in mine. "This is just my way of honoring you, your name, and everything you mean to me. I'm so fucking thankful and happy you're in my life, Jill."

"Oh my God, Ben, me too." She throws herself in my arms again, this time delivering a kiss that has me dragging her onto my lap, our breathing turning heavier as it grows more heated. I'm about to lower her to the floor when she rips her lips from mine and shakes her head back and forth.

"Not yet!" She scoots herself off of me and wags her finger at me. "You are so naughty, which normally I like." She grins wickedly. "But, first, you have to open your presents!"

After all the amazing gifts that he has just given me, I feel a little silly. I hand him a hand-carved square wooden box. It's secured shut with a tiny padlock. Ben pulls at it for a moment before looking at me with his brow raised. I chuckle and hold up the key. He reaches for it, but I pull it away. "Uh-uh, you have to listen to the story attached to this gift first," I direct with a smile.

He pulls me toward him, and I nestle up against him. "Well, let's hear it then."

"So, my grandmother and I were very close. When I was younger, she used to tell me this story about a rich woman whose heart was broken and bruised by several men. The woman became jaded and scared to love. One day, she decided she'd had enough and carved a heart from the wood of a hickory tree. She cut out her own heart and replaced it with the wooden heart. She believed that, this way, nobody else would be able to hurt her heart or bruise it, because it was made of the hardest wood."

I turn my head to look at Ben to find him staring at me with adoration. I feel my cheeks warm from this single look and turn away so I can finish the story. "One day, she meets a man, and this man didn't want her money. He didn't want her jewels. All he wanted was her love, but she was afraid she couldn't show her love because her heart was now made of wood. So, to show him that she loved him, she took her wooden heart and presented him with it, knowing he would always care for it and for her."

Now that I've shared the story with Ben, I become nervous and avoid looking him in the eye. I reach out to tentatively hand him the key and watch as he opens the box. There, on a bed of purple satin, lays a wooden heart. Ben looks at it for a second, and then his eyes flash up to mine. I bite my lip.

"Does this mean what I think it means?" he asks me.

I bob my head up and down and finally meet his gaze. "These last few months have been the best of my life, Ben. I can honestly say that I have never been this happy, ever. So, yes, it means what you think it means. I love you, Benjamin Sapphire."

He pulls me into his arms and peers into my eyes. "Thank you for giving me the best Christmas present I have ever had, Jillian Baldwin. No contest."

"Really?"

"Really." He places a kiss on my lips and gazes into my eyes. "I'll take your heart, Jill, and I'll keep it safe, because I love you, too. More than I ever thought possible."

Jill steps out of the bedroom, and I can't help but admire her with pride. She always looks amazing, but today, she's dressed entirely in white, and she looks more like an angel than ever. The pants she's wearing are loose and flowing like silk, and she's topped them with a soft cashmere sweater that falls off each shoulder, her entire neck area exposed, highlighting the necklace I gave her earlier.

I'm dressed for the day as well, and have on a charcoal gray, three-piece suit, sans tie of course, with a fitted white dress shirt. I walk to her and nod in appreciation. "If I didn't know better…"

She tilts her head and scrunches up her cute little nose. "If you didn't know what any better?"

I pull her flush to me and smooth my hand down her back. "I would swear there are wings hidden here somewhere."

She laughs and tilts her head up to me, a smile shining on her face. "And if I didn't know any better, Benjamin Sapphire, I'd think you were trying to sweet talk your way right into the bedroom again."

I grin wickedly at her and then shake my head. "As much as I would love to do that, we've run out of time. There's some place, or I guess, some thing, that I'd like to share with you."

I give her a quick squeeze before letting her go, and look down at her feet, currently clad in a pair of white heels lined with silver edging, and frown. "Do you think you could humor me and throw on a pair of boots? It will make where I want to take you much easier."

Without hesitation, she shrugs and nods her head. "Sure. Let me go see what I might have in your closet. I can't remember."

I follow her into the closet along the back wall, and slide my feet into my black leather biker boots, but I also grab a pair of dress loafers to take with me.

Jill glides up beside me, a small tote bag in hand, and takes my shoes from me and stores them in the bag with hers. She looks down at her feet and clicks the heels of her boots together, then back up at me giggling.

"Yee-haw." She's wearing a pair of black cowboy boots. "It's all I could find."

I chuckle and nod approvingly. "They'll do. At least, better than the heels you had on."

After pulling on our jackets, hats, and gloves, we take the elevator downstairs and exit into the lobby of the building. "Give me one second, okay?"

"Of course."

I unlock the door to the gym, quickly stride across the large space into the kitchen, and grab a box I've stored in the large industrial refrigerator. Then, I make my way back to Jill.

Her brows rise as she eyes the content of the box. "Um, morbid much, Ben? Wouldn't red or white roses be more fitting on Christmas?"

I look down at the bouquets of black roses stored in the box and then back at her, my lips trying to form a small smile. "I'll explain in the car. Come on." I offer her my hand, and we make our way out into the snow and down the alley where I'm parked. I help her into the car, ask her to hold the box, and then climb in on the driver's side.

The alley seems to have blocked the car from much snowfall, because the wipers clear what little snow is on the windshield and the back window is barely covered as I start the car and reverse out into the street.

I head in the direction of the parkway and then reach over to take one of Jill's hands. She's taken off her gloves, and her hand is warmer than usual in mine. She hasn't said a thing, intuitively seeming to understand that what I'm sharing with her isn't easy for me. When she sees the direction we're headed, she turns to me. "We're going to Brooklyn?"

I nod my head and figure there's no time like the present to start explaining. "Yes, to Cypress Hill Cemetery."

Her hand squeezes mine more tightly as she looks down at the flowers and then back over at me. "The military cemetery?"

"Yeah." I grip the steering wheel a little tighter in the one hand I'm holding it with and blow out a sigh. "I go there a lot."

I shake my head. "Well, probably not as much as I used to over the last few months, but always on Christmas."

"Sorry. I'm guessing that's my fault," she lets out meekly.

I squeeze her hand. "Don't apologize. Believe me, Jill, none of these guys would blame me one bit for blowing them off to spend a little more time with you."

"So, tell me about your friends." She turns in her seat so she can face me. "I want to know about them."

I turn my head and give her a loving smile. "Jesus, I know I just said this an hour ago, but damn if I'm not the luckiest bastard in the whole world."

"I'd say we both got pretty lucky." She lifts my hand to her mouth and places a soft kiss on the back of it before lowering it back to her lap.

"Well, you know, of course, about the gym, and that it's dedicated to the guys I served with. Baker and Landon were in the truck with me when we hit the explosive that took my leg. Baker was one of my closest friends, and when I woke and saw him dead next to me, it was like someone had stuck a goddamn stake into my heart. I didn't find out until after I woke up in the hospital that Landon had died as well."

I close my eyes for just a second, the pain from the memory causing my heart to contract tightly, but breathe out, trying to push it away. "I was sent home, of course. And pissed as hell, of course. Pissed my friends had died and I couldn't even go to their funerals or help their families.

Pissed I lost my leg and couldn't go back and blow those mother fuckers up. And pissed that our country didn't seem to give a flying fuck about what was happening to those still over there serving."

"So, basically, you were pissed." She chuckles lightly, and I can't help but let out a laugh in return.

"Yeah, I guess that about sums it up," I joke. "I think the worst of it for me, though, was Rose, er, Jackson; Hannah's first husband. He was actually a Marine, not Army like me, but we were all stationed in the same area, and somehow, this squirrelly little fucker got under my skin and seemed to be everywhere I was. We became friends… good friends."

"I've seen pictures of him in Grace's room. Did you know that there's one of you and him together on her dresser? You look so young in it!"

"Yeah, I actually gave that to Hannah a while back. It used to be in my office, but I don't know, it just seemed like something she should have. Hannah said she wanted Gracie to know that her daddy and her uncle were friends, so she thought her room was the best place for it."

I can feel I'm starting to get a little more than nostalgic, so I shake my head to try to clear away some of its weight.

"You okay?" Jill reaches out a hand and places it softly on my cheek. I turn my head and place a kiss on her palm and then nod. "I'm good. Just a lot of memories."

Her hand moves back to her lap, covering the one that's holding her other hand, and rests there, her fingers grazing back in forth in comfort over my skin.

"Yeah, so Jackson came back to the States on leave when Grace was born, and came to see me. I was still in the hospital healing, still angry as fuck. He was even madder than me, and was so eager to get back and, as he put it, 'get even'. I begged him to reconsider. He just had a baby, for Christ's sake. He had a beautiful wife. He had both goddamn legs. But he wouldn't listen to reason. He died a few weeks later. Killed in action."

I look over at Jill and am surprised when I see tears streaming down her face. "I'm so sorry, Ben. I wish there was some way I could take all this pain from you and carry it instead. You've lost too much already."

We're in the cemetery now, so I pull the car over and put it in park, but leave it running to keep it warm, and then pull her into my arms. This is why I love this woman so much. To want to take my pain and have it be her own. Who says things like that? Who wants to do things like that? She lives up to my nickname of Angel more every day.

I kiss her head and whisper, "I love you so much, Jill."

"I love you right back." She hugs me hard and holds on until I slowly pull us apart.

"This helps me." I lift my hand and point a finger out my windshield toward the gravestones in front of us. "Coming here. Honoring them. Making sure they know I'll never forget them or what they meant to me, to this country."

"And the black roses?" She looks down at the box she placed on the floor between her legs some time ago.

I point to the tattoo on my arm. "A few of us got these to honor Baker, Landon, and Jackson. The rose specifically for Jackson, and well, you know all about my black heart." I shrug.

"I know all about your heart, Ben, and it's nowhere near black."

I look at her and smile. "Not anymore."

She goes with me then, and we walk through the cemetery, stopping at the grave of each of my friends, my brothers, as we place a bouquet of the roses on each their stones. I tell her a little more about each of them. Hannah is the only other person I've brought here, but Jill is the only one who has ever made my heart feel lighter while doing so.

An hour later, we pull back into the alley and park the car. We run up to the loft and grab three big bags of presents and a couple bottles of wine, and then head back outside. The snow is still falling gently, so we decide to leave our boots on and just walk the block over to Drew and Hannah's place.

Jill tries to catch snowflakes on her tongue as we walk, and I think my cheeks might actually crack if my smile grows any wider as I watch.

We reach the building in minutes and stomp the snow off our feet as we enter the lobby and share Christmas greetings with the doorman. He knows us by name, our familiarity a product of the frequent visits we both make here.

When we step off the elevator, Gracie is already standing in the hallway waiting for us, arms thrown wide as she runs over and hugs us both. "Merry Christmas, Uncle Benny and Jill!"

I drop the bags and scoop her up in my arms, swinging her around before giving her a large hug. When I look up, I see my mom standing in the doorway to the apartment, a very content Brody on her hip, sucking on a green candy cane.

"Merry Christmas, Mom." I smile and set Grace on the ground so I can retrieve the bags and enter the house. I give my mom a one-armed hug and watch with warmth as Jill hugs her with both.

"You two are all covered in snow." My mom already beginning her fussing. "Put those bags right there and take off those wet shoes and coats before you come in any further. Hannah will have a fit if you dirty up her floors."

"What will I have a fit about?" Hannah strolls in carrying a large tray of cut vegetables, placing them down on a table before moving over to give Jill and I a hug. "Merry Christmas, you two."

She takes a step back, places a hand on her hip, and cocks her head at us. "You two are practically glowing. Any news you want to share?"

She glances toward Jill's left hand and lifts her brows in hope. Jill's eyes pop wide, and her head begins shaking back and forth. "Oh God, no! Hannah!"

She slaps at her playfully and then lays her hand flat against her breast bone under the necklace I gave her. "I mean, wouldn't you be glowing if Drew had your name put in diamonds?"

That's all it takes for all three women to gather round and start chatting about presents and shoes, and whatever it is women go off and talk in circles about. I chuckle as they all head off in the direction of the kitchen, and then look down when I hear crinkling behind me.

"Gracie, what are you doing?" Her little blonde head pops out of the bag, her wide eyes meeting mine.

"Nothing, Uncle Benny. Just looking to see which presents are mine." She starts bouncing up and down in place, and I can't help but laugh out loud when I realize she's the spitting image of Jill a few hours ago.

"Well, let's go find Dad and Grandpa and see if we can't gather the troops so we can open these puppies up. Sound good?"

"You got me a puppy?" Her eyes light up as her face widens in delight, and I freeze in place.

I let out a long sigh and realize it's going to be a very long day as I try to explain my choice of words. I wonder where the hell my brother is hiding because I need his help pronto. And, damn if I wasn't ready for a Christmas drink, too.

We spend the next few hours opening presents, well, Gracie doing most of the present opening, and then have a wonderful dinner together. I realize as I look around the table, surrounded by the people who mean the most to me, who I love the most, that I may just be the luckiest man alive. And for the first time in a really long time, I don't feel guilty anymore for being the one that survived.

I smile over at Jill and take her hand into mine and

squeeze it softly. "Thank you for the most amazing Christmas I've had in a long time."

"You're so welcome." She raises her eyebrows and smiles wide.

One Week Later...

My eyes flutter open, and I lift my head off the pillow to look down to try to figure out what's woken me up. One side of my mouth cocks up when I see the top of Jill's head hovering over my stomach, her finger tracing over the lines of one of my tattoos. "Morning, beautiful."

She hums as she places a soft kiss against my chest. "Morning."

"Whatcha doing down there? Come give me a proper kiss," I growl, reaching to pull her up.

"I don't think I've gotten to know this one yet." She pushes my hand away and continues moving her finger lazily over my lower abdomen.

I chuckle softly and move my hand to rest it in her hair instead. I know where this is headed, and I have absolutely no intention of interrupting her. "Angel, I think you know all my tattoos pretty well by now, but by all means, investigate further if you must."

She raises her head just enough so she can peek up at me under her lashes, licking her lips as she flashes me a very sexy smile, and then leans back over me, replacing her finger with her tongue. My head falls back against the pillow, and I close my eyes, letting myself bask in the attention she's giving me right now.

I feel her tongue lift off my skin and then the vibration of her voice as she speaks. "I don't think I ever noticed the way these feathers curve up here around this muscle." And then her tongue is back against my skin, the tip dragging along the edge of one of my lower muscles, and then lower still, my skin breaking out in goosebumps as she goes.

"Last time I checked, there wasn't any ink below my waist, love," I murmur, but don't hesitate to lift my hips when her hands make quick work of removing my boxers.

"Shhh, I'm just looking to make sure." Her fingers trail up my stomach and then rake back down slowly, stopping when they circle around the base of my cock and tighten, her tongue dragging up its hard length, and then her hot, wet mouth sliding down to cover me.

My hips thrust up involuntarily, and a loud moan rolls up from my chest. *Now, this is a great fucking way to wake up.* My hands find her head, and I tangle my fingers in her downy locks, helping to guide her up and down as she sucks me in and swirls her tongue around me, my cock growing even harder. She moans and the vibration against my cock almost causes me to explode right then and there.

I tighten my grip in her hair and pull her off me with a soft pop, guiding her back up my body. When she's close enough, I slam my lips against hers and yank her body flush to mine. She's naked, and her hard nipples brush against mine as she adjusts herself over me. She thinks she's in control, and for a moment, I let her believe it as she slides her wet center up and down my throbbing length.

When she shifts to move higher so she can impale herself with my cock, I grab her arms and roll over, trapping her beneath me, a small gasp falling from her parted mouth as her wide eyes look up at me. "You don't think I'm going to let you do that yet, do you?"

Her teeth find her lower lip and she bites it, as if trying to quench the obvious hunger stirring within, shaking her head softly. I don't give her a chance to reply verbally, because I crush my mouth to hers, my tongue twisting with hers, her body pushing back against mine in desperation. She wraps a leg around me and tries to rock her center against my cock, but I release her lips and slide down her body, effectively breaking the hold she has, and suck one taut peak into my mouth.

I smile around the nipple when I feel her hands clutch the sheets next to me and hear a moan from above. My minx is on fire, and my lips on her only seem to fan the flames higher.

I release her hard bud, run my tongue over it with one hard swipe, and then rake a wet trail down her stomach until I reach the apex of her legs. Without hesitation, her legs fall open wide in invitation and I enter greedily, plunging my tongue into her sweet core. I stroke softly until

I land against her hard nub and then wrap my lips around her and suck.

Her hands are instantly in my hair, clutching wildly, her knees rising to push her feet into the bed as I grasp her hips tightly and suck even harder. "Oh my God, Ben. I'm going to come if you don't stop."

I want her to come, I do, all over my goddamn face, but I want her pulsing around my cock even more, so I release her and move like lightening up her body and between her legs. Her hands move to my arms, her nails digging into me as she clings to me, and I lean over and slowly ease myself into her. Her hot walls clench and then pulse, pulling me in deeper, holding tightly as I arch my back and plunge all the way in.

We both groan when my center slams against her, and I still, but only for a moment before I slide back out and then drive back into her again.

"Oh my God, yes. Harder, Ben!" I need no further encouragement and surge back and forth against her body, thrusting my cock as deep as it will go, my arms flexed tightly as I hold myself over her.

After only a few moments, I feel her tighten around my cock like a blood pressure cuff, her head thrashing back and forth on the pillow, her hands reaching out to grasp me around the neck. She lets out a long, guttural moan, followed by my name in a whisper.

As if it was even possible, hearing my name from her pink lips causes my blood to surge straight to my cock, turning it to stone. I move faster now, my hips pummeling against hers as I feel my balls tighten and then finally explode, my release coating her insides. I clutch onto her, pulling her flat against me, my hot breaths against her ear as I moan out her name again and again.

When my pulse finally slows down enough for me to think reasonably, I roll off her and lay flat on my back, my breaths still coming out in pants. *Holy fuck. How in the world does this just keep getting better and better?*

She lifts herself and lays the top half of her body across my chest, her hand under her chin as she looks up at me. "Did I say good morning yet?" And then she breaks into a fit of giggles as her face flushes a beautiful shade of pink.

An hour later, we're both showered and in the kitchen. I'm drinking a cup of coffee as I watch her move around, cooking for us. She's humming and moving her hips softly to the rhythm, and I realize I could never feel more content. "Move in with me."

She freezes, spatula suspended in mid-air, and turns to me, eyes wide, her mouth forming a small 'O' shape before finally speaking.

"What?"

"Move in with me." I set my mug on the counter and move closer to her.

I slide the spatula from her fingers and wrap my arms around her. "You're here all the time anyway now."

"Ben…" Her face scrunches up in thought for a second. "I mean, I don't know. What about Mik?"

"What about Mik?" I counter. "She's a big girl. And Rae is right across the hall from her. I'm quite sure she'll be just fine."

She chews on her lip in contemplation, and I can tell there are a hundred thoughts swirling around in her head.

"Listen, just think about it, okay?" Her head nods up and down, her expression dazed.

I tug her closer to me. "Jill, I love you. I love having you here. I love waking up with you every day. I didn't mean to freak you out or scare you."

"I'm not scared." She peeks up at me. "Nothing has ever felt more right to me."

"Really?" I can't help the smile that spreads across my face.

"Really." She nods again, almost like she can't believe what she's saying. "I just have to figure out how I'm going to tell the girls."

"So, you're moving in? That's a yes?" I have a hard time containing the joy in my voice, but I don't give a shit. It gives me a sense of relief and anticipation knowing what else I have planned for her tonight.

Her face breaks into a huge smile. "It's a yes."

"Woohoo!" I tighten my arms around her and swing her around in a large circle, crushing my lips to hers in delight. She squeals out in laughter and then slaps at my arms to put her down.

"Ben, put me down! I have to finish breakfast."

Her cheeks are flushed and I know, even though she's trying to play it cool, she's just as excited as me for this next step. "If I'm not at Rae and Mik's by eleven, they will kill me. You know how they feel about preparations."

"Well, if this is the start to our New Year, I think it's going to be fucking amazing." I plant one more kiss on her cheek and let her go so she can finish cooking. "So, what does that crazy duo have in store for you this time?"

"Oh, you know them… Of course, the entire afternoon will be spent at the spa. My rules, not theirs. There's no way I'm showing up to your charity event tonight looking anything less than fabulous."

"Angel, you could show up in a plastic bag and I'd still think you were the most gorgeous woman in the world." I slap her ass playfully and wink.

"You, Benjamin Sapphire, are biased." She turns and smiles sweetly at me. "But thank you. After the spa, we're going to go to my place for dressing. Mik has designed some stunning new creations for us to wear. I can't wait to see them!"

"And I can't wait to see you in it." I raise my brows suggestively.

"You're insatiable!" She grins back. "Are you sure you don't mind me meeting you at the event? It's just going to be so much easier riding over with Mik and the gang instead of coming all the way back over here."

I move up behind her, wrapping her in my arms, and lean my head down on hers. "I told you already, it's fine. It's good, actually, because I have a ton of stuff I need to do before the event. Need to make sure all ducks are in a row and what not."

She spins in my arms, throwing hers around my neck, and smiles up at me. "I love you, Benjamin. I know I tell you all the time now, but I do. I just want you to know that. And I'm still so glad every day that you chased after my stubborn ass."

I soften at her words, knowing without a doubt that everything I have planned for this evening is happening at the perfect time. "I love you, too, Jill." And I kiss her, hoping to show her just how much.

CHAPTER

Fifteen

After we have spent the entire day at the spa getting pampered, we arrive at the penthouse with the girls in full-blown party mode. I go to my room, take a quick shower, and then head to Mik's dressing room to see what kind of magic she's created for me. I walk in just in time to hear the cork pop.

"Jillybean!" They greet me in unison.

"Hey girls." I stroll in wearing my robe, a smile on my face.

Raeva hands me a glass of champagne, smiling like the Cheshire cat.

"What's with the face breaking smile?" I ask with a chuckle.

"I'm just excited about tonight. Whoever came up with the idea for this party is brilliant. Oh, and wait until you see what Mikaela has got for us to wear tonight."

I don't even have to see the outfits to know they will be

spectacular. Everything Mik designs is fabulous. It's New Year's Eve, and we're going to a party being held at the Sapphire Resort; the very one I met Ben in, which seems like such a good omen to the start of our night and the year ahead.

Someone came up with the amazing concept of working the party into a charity. Every guest must donate money into a pot in order to attend. The guests then divide into teams for a scavenger hunt, with the winning team getting to choose the charity they want the total funds donated to. Not only does it sound like fun, but we get to help a good cause.

"Is Ben meeting us here?" Mik asks.

I shake my head and take a sip of the champagne. "No, he said he had tons to take care of for the event and that it would be easier for him to just meet us there."

"Ah. Okay, well, when he sees you, he might not get up."

I frown. "I'm sorry… what?"

Mikaela rolls her eyes. "Because you'll look so amazing; you'll knock him out. Duh."

Raeva and I burst out laughing. "You're a nut, Mik."

She smirks and holds out a hanger with a gorgeous black sequin dress. The dress has a rounded neckline, with a scoop back and three-quarter sleeves. And, it's short, falling a good four inches above my knee making it incredibly sexy.

Ben loves when I show some leg. Of course, it fits like a glove. Mikaela is a magician when it comes to things like this. She knows exactly what looks good on anyone or anything.

"You will need a pair of amazing shoes to go with that, of course," Rae chimes in. "Lucky for you, your person has just acquired these."

She passes me a shoebox, and my brows rise in delight when I read Jimmy Choo on the box and know they are going to be fancy. I lift the lid and gasp. Inside, I find a pair of black and silver, coarse-glitter-covered, pointy toe pumps. They are perfect. I hug my friends and thank them.

I start to work on my make-up, and watch in the mirror as Rae and Mik begin dressing, all of us continuing to chat about this and that. Mikaela is wearing her signature gold. The color matches her eyes, and she looks stunning. Raeva is dressed in a gorgeous silk top and pant set.

I do make-up and hair for each of us. Mika must be getting impatient for our company, because he's already sent three texts in the last twenty minutes. We take the final one as our queue to leave and all rise and take one last look in the mirror.

We squeeze each other's hands and look expectantly at each other before I finally speak. "I think we're ready, girls." We all nod in agreement and leave the dressing room to head to the party.

Once downstairs, we climb into a gorgeous white limo and head to the financial district. I pull my phone out of my purse, check the screen, and frown. Still nothing from Ben. It's a bit strange, as he usually checks in, but I try not to think too much about it, knowing he had so much to do to prepare for the event. I'll see him very soon and can't wait for him to see me in Mik's latest creation.

I've been wondering all day how I am going to tell Mik that I am moving in with Ben. I know she will be happy for me, but I hate the thought of her being alone in that big place.

I know I've spent almost every night since meeting Ben at his place anyway, but I still can't help but feel bad. I know she's lonely, especially in the evenings, when she's wishing she could be with Eric.

When we pull up in front of the building, a large smile breaks across my face as my mind drifts back to all those months ago—the night Ben picked me out of the crowd, my knight in shining armor, even if I didn't know it then, at the opening gala for the hotel. I shake my head when I recall my unwillingness to even have a drink with the man, and whom I now can't imagine being without.

We head into the lobby where we are all greeted and directed to the coat check. I scan the room for Ben, but still see no sign of him. We make our way to the large ballroom on the second floor as a group and marvel at the opulence before us. The room is gorgeously decorated with flowers dipped in glitter scattered throughout and candles burning on every surface. After securing drinks at the bar, we find our table and take our seats.

A staff member gets on the small stage in the center of the room and begins the evening by requesting our donations and then directing us to a list containing the name of our assigned team mates. Of course, because I know some strings must have been pulled, my team consists of Hannah, Mikaela, Raeva, and of course, myself.

The rules are explained again, and we each listen intently. Each team has until midnight to try to solve the clues provided to them. Each clue will lead to the next and so on until we get to the last one. The first team to get to the last clue will get to pick the charity of their choice to donate the combined money to. We are instructed to assign a team captain, and without hesitation, Raeva gets the job with a unanimous vote.

"Okay, first things first," Rae says, holding a little card. "According to this, we have to declare our charity before we start. Any suggestions?"

"Get Vets Set!" Hannah and I say in unison.

We look at each other in surprise and then giggle.

"It's Ben's charity." I explain. "He offers free gym memberships and physical therapy for vets. It is such a great initiative, and I would love it if we would support him."

"I second that," Hannah chimes in.

"I'm three for three," Mik says with a grin.

"Get Vets Set, it is!"

Raeva fills out the card and hands it in, and we receive our very first clue. It's a balloon. There are some numbers and letters written on the face of it, but they don't make sense; P4P M2 T4 S22 WH1T C4M2S N2XT. Attached to the balloon is a little card that says:

A = 1

E = 2

I = 3

O = 4

U = 5

We stare at the balloon and the card for a moment.

"Ohhh," Rae exclaims as she pulls a pin from her hair. "Pop me to see what comes next!" She stabs the pin into the balloon.

A little note falls out, and I pick it up, unfold it, and read it out loud. "In order to find the next clue, you will have to go to the front desk and ask for something. To find out what to ask for, solve this riddle: I have cities, but no houses. I have mountains, but no trees. I have water, but no fish. What am I?"

I'm glad I've only had one glass of champagne, because apparently, we are going to need our thinking caps on tonight. I repeat the words and mull them over in my head. Then, I remember a few weeks ago, while Ben and I were visiting Drew, Hannah, and the kids, Gracie made Ben and me watch this cartoon with her. What were the odds?

"I know what it is!" I exclaim, and motion for them to follow me as I make a beeline for the front desk. The others don't hesitate and follow. When we make it to the front desk, I approach the young lady behind the counter and give her one of my brightest smiles. "Excuse me, um," I look at her name tag, "Gloria, would you by any chance have a map?"

Gloria beams and nods her head in delight. "Certainly, ma'am. Just a moment."

She bends behind the counter for just a second, and then pops up, holding a map of the hotel in her hands. She passes it over to us, and we open it, noting there is a route highlighted. We thank Gloria and start to figure out where we are on the map.

We follow the highlighted path and end up in a small room with a table set up in the middle of it. The table has a beautiful hand-painted silk table cloth, and on top of the table are twelve different desserts, a pitcher of water, and a dozen water glasses. Next to the pitcher sits a little locked black box, and next to that, tied to a little holder on the table, is another balloon.

Raeva pulls the pin back out of her hair and pops the balloon. Another note drops, and Mikaela picks it up and unfolds it. "One of these yummy desserts holds the key."

The key? To the box?

"Well, ladies, let's dig in," Hannah says as she grabs a fork.

"I call dibs on the crème brûlée!" Rae says as she lunges toward her favorite dessert with gusto.

"I'll guess I'll go for this lava cake," Mik announces.

I myself am about to dig into a huge piece of triple chocolate cake when Hannah announces that she has the key. It's covered in frosting, though, so Mikaela pours some water in a glass and drops the key in it. We fish it back out, clean it off, and then open the box. Inside the box is yet another clue.

"A woman shoots her husband, then holds him underwater for five minutes. Next, she hangs him. Right after, they enjoy a lovely dinner. Explain."

The four of us look at each other before a giggling fit ensues.

"Nice lady," Hannah chuckles.

"Oh my God, I know what this means!"

We all look expectantly at Mikaela.

"Listen, when I was in school and had time for hobbies, I used to love to take pictures. Never digital, though. I was an old-fashioned girl—except when it came to clothes, of course," she says with a wink. "Anyway," she continues, "all of it can be explained. We need to find a picture or a darkroom or both. Hannah, does this resort have one?"

"Honestly? I am not sure. The resorts are Drew's territory."

"Wait," Rae says. "The map!"

Sure enough, when we unfold the map, we find that the resort does indeed have a darkroom. We head there immediately.

The darkroom is located below ground level, so we take the elevator down and are relieved to find the room unlocked. But the red light outside is on, which means we can't go in. Fortunately, there is a balloon tied to the doorknob. We pop it, and once more, a note falls to the floor, but also four keys.

"A picture speaks a thousand words. But only one key works."

Each key has a keychain on it that reads a different direction. North, East, South, and West. Hmmm. Cryptic. We knock but get no response.

"Oh, screw it," I tell my friends. "I'm going in."

My friends reluctantly follow me into the darkroom, which is just that, dark. Besides the red glow that illuminates the room, it is devoid of brightness, but we notice there are several pictures hanging from a line.

I step forward and inspect the images. On every picture, there is a terrace, and it looks to be the same terrace. In the middle of the terrace, tied to something is a balloon.

"I know where this is!" Hannah says excitedly. "It's the roof top terrace. There are four entrances, and I think one of these keys will open a door. Only thing is, I have no idea which. I say, if we want to win this thing, we need to split up."

"Yes, great idea," Mikaela chimes in. "There are four keys and four of us. We will split up, and whoever opens the door first and finds the balloon will call the others. Sound good?"

I am totally good with that. I really want to win the donation money for Ben's charity. Raeva divides the keys. She gives Hannah South, Mik West, me North, and she heads to the East. We all take the elevator to the top floor before splitting up.

On the top floor, there is a small stairwell that leads to the roof terrace. I head to my particular stairwell and climb up until I reach the door. I insert the key and squeal with glee when I attempt to turn the knob and it actually works.

I push the door open and step onto the terrace. When I do, I am mesmerized, my mouth falling open at the beauty before me. There are literally an ocean's worth of white lilies and candles spread on every surface. It is absolutely breathtaking, and I marvel at it a moment in silence.

Even the chilly December wind that brushes across my skin with its icy touch isn't a deterrent, and I move forward to investigate. I walk further onto the terrace and spot the balloon. I stride toward it with tunnel vision.

I stop, because I realize that I have no pin. I look at the balloon and frown for a moment. A smile tugs at my lips when I realize I have something else I can use; a pen that I stuck in my purse after I wrote the donation check down-stairs. I fish it out and pop the balloon, my face lighting up in victory.

Unlike with the other balloons, this time, there is a loud thud as something drops to the floor. I look down, pick it up, and stare at it. It is a small black heart, made from some type of stone. I'm turning it in my hand when I'm startled by a familiar voice behind me.

"My angel, so resourceful."

I turn and see my gorgeous man sauntering toward me. He is wearing a three-piece black suit that is so perfect on him that I swear it has been sewed onto him. Ben always looks hot, but by God, when he wears a suit, he just blows me away. Every. Single. Time.

"Ben! You're finally here. You missed all the fun," I tell him regretfully.

"I have not missed a thing. Except maybe you," he tells me as he kisses the tip of my nose. "You look beautiful, Angel, but you must be cold." He shrugs out of his jacket and places it over my shoulders.

"What ya got there?" he asks as he nudges the heart clutched tightly in my hand.

"Oh this is—" I stop talking as the light bulb in my head finally goes on. Of course, a black heart.

Ben sees the recognition in my eyes because he lights up and cups my face. "Angel, what you're holding there so tightly in your beautiful hand is everything that I was, everything that I thought I would always be, and everything you changed with your love. For years, my heart has been black and cold as stone."

I look at him and shake my head softly because I know his heart is anything but cold, and I take my free hand and grip one of his in mine. I nod as he continues.

"I didn't think anyone would be able to love a man like me; broken, angry and cold. But since the very first time I laid eyes on you, I began to feel myself start to thaw. And, as time went on, I realized you had thawed it completely. I no longer prefer the darkness, because you are the light. You brightened my life by being the amazing person you are."

He looks down at his legs and then back into my eyes. "I have not felt whole since I lost my leg. But, Angel, you make me feel as if I have a thousand legs. You make me feel like, leg or no leg, the man I am now, with you, is more whole and complete and a better version of what I was even before my accident. I don't want to wake up another day without you next to me. I don't want to wake up another day without being able to call you mine—officially and legally. So, I am standing here before you, the man that you have made whole, asking you to please consider being mine forever. Give me a chance to brighten your life as you do mine. If you say yes, I promise that I will spend every waking moment of my life trying to make you happy, trying to make you smile, and most definitely loving you in every way you deserve, every single day for the rest of our lives."

Tears are streaming down my face as I watch Ben sink to one knee and present me with a box. "Jillian Baldwin, will you marry me?"

He opens the box to reveal the most beautiful ring I have ever seen, glittering up at me as it sits on a pillow of white satin. The center stone is a large, round black diamond with a white diamond halo surrounding it. The band itself is lined with little black diamonds and is stunning. It is so perfect for us.

I am staring at the ring, sobbing and clutching on to the final clue—my little black stone heart. I'm overwhelmed and speechless and just keep looking from the ring back to Ben.

"Angel, you're kind of leaving me hanging here," he mumbles a little nervously.

I drop to my knees in front of him and cup his face in my free hand.

"There isn't anything I want more in this world than to spend the rest of my life with you. You already own me, Ben. We don't need a ring for that. But, yes, yes! I will marry you! Being your wife, being yours, nothing could make me happier!"

I lean in and our lips crash together, sealing our promise with a kiss. After a few seconds, he pulls back, grins broadly, and then lets out a roar. "She said yes!"

All the doors surrounding the terrace fly open, and the place starts to swarm with our friends and loved ones. I have barely made it back onto my feet when I nearly get tackled by Raeva. She is crying her eyes out. "I can't believe you're getting married," she sobs. "I am so happy. Congratulations."

"Hey, stop hogging the bride-to-be!" Mik jokes as she puts her arms around us both and squeezes tight.

"Show us the ring!" Hannah says excitedly as she joins us.

"Did you guys know about this?" I ask, although, I already know the answer.

"Guilty," Raeva admits.

"Yup, me too," Mikaela says

"I guess that makes me three." Hannah beams.

"Well, girls, thank you for helping Ben make tonight unforgettable," I say with a genuine smile.

We are congratulated by all our family and friends, and I'm completely surprised when I see my mom and dad appear in front of me. Apparently, Ben actually went and asked my dad for my hand in marriage, much to their delight, and he happily said yes.

We eat, drink, and celebrate our new engagement. Just a few minutes before midnight, Ben takes me by the arm and leads me to the edge of the roof terrace. His arm snakes around my waist, and he pulls me close as we look upon the New York skyline. The view up here is breathtaking.

He leans down and looks into my eyes. "Were you surprised tonight?"

I smile. "I don't think I have ever been more surprised," I tell him with a smile.

"Good," he says, pleased. "I will continue to try and surprise you for the rest of our lives."

"I will continue to love that," I reply.

Ben kisses the top of my head. "On that note, I have one more surprise for you."

I turn to face him. "You're pregnant?"

Ben chuckles. "Not yet, Angel."

"Oh, that's disappointing," I say with a wink.

"I'm pretty sure we can practice making a baby a little later tonight, though, if you'd like."

Just the promise of seeing him naked has heat pooling between my thighs, and I bite my lip in anticipation. I know Ben has noticed because that cocky smirk on his face says it all. I catch his gaze and marvel for a moment at the beauty of his eyes. If eyes are truly the windows to the soul, then right now, his windows are wide open.

He's completely bared himself to me, and I to him; this man who I will spend the rest of my life adoring. Behind us, people start the count down the time to midnight, but we continue to look in each other's eyes.

Ten… nine… eight… seven… six… five… four… three…

"I love you," he whispers as he leans in to take my lips.

…Two… "I love you, too."

…One…

HAPPY NEW YEAR!

Five Months Later

I clasp my hands nervously in front of me, turning my head to look at my brother standing beside me. It wasn't that long ago that our roles were reversed, and I was standing where he is now. How completely different it feels to know that my angel, my Jill, will be walking down this aisle any second to become my wife.

No sooner than that thought crosses my mind, the traditional wedding march song starts, and my heart, already beating faster than normal, stampedes against my chest like a herd of wild horses.

I see the first glimmer of white as she steps through the arch of flowers at the end of the short aisle, breath stuck in my throat when she finally comes fully into view, and gasp at how stunningly perfect she looks.

I want so badly to look into her eyes, to see and have her

see how much love exists right now, in this very moment between us, but her face his hidden behind a delicate lace veil.

"You're a lucky man, Benny." Drew whispers into my ear, his hand coming up to grip my shoulder.

"God damn right I am." I whisper back, still staring in awe at the vision walking toward me.

My eyes sweep down the elegant dress she's wearing, and then back up to her face, where I can see her smiling, even through the lace, now that's she getting closer.

After what I know has only been a minute, possibly two, my bride-to-be finally comes to a stop beside me. She releases one hand from the bouquet of white lilies she's holding, and slides it into my waiting one as she looks over at me. "Fancy meeting you here."

I chuckle, unable to control the happiness coursing through me, smiling broadly at her in return. "I heard you were going to be here." I shrug, trying to be nonchalant, but fail miserably when I can't wipe the smile from my face. I lean toward her then and ever so softly whisper, "You look so beautiful my angel."

"Ladies and gentleman," the priest begins to speak, interrupting any other interaction between Jill and I. "Thank you so much for being here to witness this blessed union of Jill Baldwin and Benjamin Michael Sapphire on this fifth day of May, two-thousand eighteen."

Jill's hand squeezes mine, her head turning slightly to look at me, her smile vibrant through the lace, and I know without a doubt that doing this; marrying her, is the absolute most right thing I've ever done in my life, and I squeeze her hand right back hoping it carries with it everything I'm feeling.

"Benjamin, Jill," the priest addresses us both, "I understand you have your own vows you would like to say to each other?"

I nod my head, Jill and I both answering yes in unison.

"Will you please turn and face each other and join your hands together?"

I watch as Jill passes her bouquet to Rae, who is standing to her left and then turns to face me, slipping both of her small hands into my larger ones.

"Benjamin, please proceed when you're ready."

I thought this would be so much harder to do when the time came. I thought finding the words to say, to describe how I feel about her, our love, our life together would be difficult. Standing here before her though, her fingers clasped in mine, her heart given completely to mine, I find they come as naturally as water flowing down a stream after a spring rain.

I clear my throat and begin to speak. "Jill, on this day, which will now be the happiest of all my days up until this point in my life, I take you to be my wife. I give you my heart as I give you my hands. The heart that is only whole again because of your love. I pledge my undying love, my devotion, my very soul to you as I join my life with yours. Wherever our journey leads, I will always be by your side, living, learning, loving, together. Forever. I love you so much."

"I love you too." She whispers in response, her hands

clutching more tightly onto mine as I watch her lids blinking rapidly under her veil.

"Jill, please proceed with your vows when you're ready."

She nods her head and then looks straight at me. "Ben, standing here in front of you and all the people we love so dearly, I promise to love you forever and am so honored to take you as my husband. I look forward to spending my days living with you, laughing with you, growing with you, and will cherish and carry your heart in mine for eternity. I started by calling you my boyfriend, and then my fiancé, and now, on this most perfect of days, I vow to love you forever as I get to call you my husband."

I want to sweep her up in my arms this very instant and crush my lips to hers, sealing our vows, and as I move forward to do just that, the priest grabs onto my arm to hold me back.

"Let's exchange rings first, shall we?" He lets out a small laugh as I take a step back, nodding.

Drew taps me on the shoulder, placing Jill's ring into the palm of my hand when I turn to him. "Almost done," he smiles at me knowingly.

I listen as the priest makes a speech about the importance of the rings, but can only focus on Jill, the rest of the world around me fading away. I watch as her lips lift into a smile and then as she mouths, *'pay attention'*, a soft giggle floating up under the lace.

"Ben, please place the ring you've selected for Jill on her left ring finger."

I take Jill's graceful hand in my calloused one, and place

the band onto her slender finger and begin sliding it down its length as I speak. "Jill, I give you this ring to wear with love and joy. As this ring has no end, neither shall my love for you. I choose you to be my wife this day and forever more."

As I slide the ring completely on, she sniffles and then clasps her fingers with mine. "It's so beautiful Ben."

She looks at me and then down at the ring, an eternity style, with black and white diamonds around the entire band. As soon as I saw it, I knew it would go perfectly with the engagement ring she already had.

"Jill, it's your turn to present your groom with the ring you've chosen."

I watch as Raeva hands her a ring, and then hold my hand out, her shaky fingers sliding the ring over my large finger. "Ben, I give you this ring as a symbol of my love and commitment for all the days of our lives. I choose you to my husband this day and forever more." She pushes the plain, quarter-inch, black platinum band all the way home and then looks up at me, a beaming smile on her face.

And finally, finally the words I've been waiting to hear. "It's my honor to now pronounce you husband and wife. Benjamin, you may kiss your bride."

I take a step forward, and using my fingers, lift the lace away from my angel's tear streaked face, then sweep her into my arms as I crush my lips against hers in a claiming kiss.

Her arms wrap around my neck, her fingers latching onto my nape as she presses against me, kissing me back with equal fervor. After a moment, and to a chorus of cheers from our friends, we finally break apart, but remain connected, our hands still joined tightly.

"Ladies and Gentleman, it is with great pleasure that I present Mr. & Mrs. Benjamin Sapphire!"

It feels like a dream. The most wonderful of dreams. And I never want this moment to end. I look around at how amazing everything and everyone looks. My cheeks hurt from smiling so much, but I don't care because I don't think I'll ever be able to wipe this smile off my face.

I am married to the man that is my entire universe, and I cannot imagine that there is a human being on this little planet made of dust and dirt, that is happier than I am, right here, right now.

The roof top looks amazing, and how fitting is it that we are getting married on the rooftop of a Sapphire Resort property; it's where we met after all.

The gown that Mikaela designed and made for me is fit for a queen. The dress has a bodice with amazing lace details and is tied with criss-crosses of silk ribbon up the back. The skirt looks like I am standing in waves of silk with a long train behind me.

I look up at my husband, my chest tightening at the realization that he's officially and legally mine now.

"You ready, Mrs. Sapphire?"

A feeling of euphoria washes over me when I hear him

call me that. "With you by my side, always Mr. Sapphire." I reply with a smile.

We make our way to the gorgeous table that has been set up for us. I have been so busy all day with preparations for the wedding, I have not eaten a single bite, and can't wait to sit down.

We eat, drink, laugh and conversation flows freely while sharing this monumental time with some of our most favorite people. I'm eating with one hand, my other seemingly fused together with Ben's since the moment we said I do.

At some point, the band starts to play, and we're introduced for our first dance. We smile at each other and rise to our feet. Ben leads me to the dance floor and pulls me close against him, gently swaying me to the music. He leans down and kisses the tip of my nose.

"Are you happy?" I ask him.

"I am." He sighs contently. "But I'll be even happier when I can get you alone. I can't believe you made me sleep at Drew's last night." He gleams down at me. "One night away from you is one night too many."

He kisses me then. A gentle kiss, but one that's full of love and promises. He slides his lips from mine, moving them against my ear, his breath hot as he whispers, "And wife, no matter how perfect you look in this dress, I can not wait to peel it off of you."

"And I can't wait for you to peel it off of me." I admit breathily. I almost combust on the spot, desire coursing through my veins, every inch of my body feeling like it's on fire. I know this man practices what he preaches, and can't wait for him to get his hands on me. I glance over at our friends, who are all watching us with smiles on their faces.

"Are you thinking what I am thinking?" I ask as our eyes meet.

"Oh Angel, I fucking hope so."

We managed to stay for nearly another hour, but I think I can safely speak for us both that it was torture. As soon as we were able to escape, we headed straight to our waiting honeymoon suite.

Butterflies danced in my belly, my desire for Ben so overwhelming, never having wanted him as much as I do right now. Is this what marriage does to someone?

The second we crossed the threshold into the room, our bodies fuse together, our lips crashing together. Tongues are dancing, hands are greedily exploring. Ben is powerful, intense, fierce. We are both totally consumed by our desire.

"Bedroom." He growls. We clumsily stumble our way through the living room, finally making our way into the bedroom. Ben pulls away and turns me around. He gently brushes my hair to the side, his breath hot against my neck as he whispers, "time to peel you out of this, Angel."

Agonizingly slow, he starts to undo the ribbon. His mouth caresses my shoulder, and when he gently bites, I nearly lose my mind. He whispers the dirtiest things as his fingers continue their quest to release me from this dress, heat pooling between my thighs. I let out a moan, and if I thought it would help, I would beg him to go faster.

He finally tugs at my gown, loose enough that it falls down my body until I'm standing in the pool of my dress wearing nothing but my stilettos and white panties. He whips me around to face him before pushing me down onto the bed. I bite my lip. The butterflies that were fluttering inside of my just a moment ago have flown away and have been replaced by fire burning in my belly.

Not taking his eyes off me once, Ben rids himself of his clothing and gets onto the bed, his eyes burning with a virile hunger. He removes his leg and prowls closer to me. He watches as my hand slides into my panties, a harsh breath sucked into his lungs as his eyes widen.

"I want to see." He tells me huskily as he reaches forward to rip the panties apart.

He licks his lips as he watches me plunge two digits into my core. He pushes my legs further apart, his eyes glued to my center, then suddenly tugs my hand away, moving lightning fast toward my core.

He takes my soaking fingers into his mouth and sucks without holding back. He throws my leg over his shoulder, his mouth connecting with my throbbing center, and begins lapping at my most intimate part, as if he's a parched man drinking from a well.

When he takes that bundle of nerves between his lips and sucks, I feel like I am slowly disintegrating with pleasure. I buck up off the bed, the stubble of his short beard rubbing against my thighs as his cheeks rise into a smile between my legs. He continues to lick, nibble and suck at me in earnest, the sweet pressure of my impending release building. And then he plunges two fingers inside of my walls, pumping them in a rapid pace, making beckoning motions as he exits.

I explode, screaming his name, over and over, like a mantra as my orgasm overtakes me. My entire body is on total meltdown, and I swear it feels like every neuron in my brain has melted and is going to pour out of my ears any moment.

"Ben, please. I need you inside of me."

His eyes shine brightly at my words, the fiery look in his eyes making me feel like prey that just has been spotted by a predator. He grins and before I can even blink, he's on top of me, positioning himself at my entrance.

"Oh Angel, I love to hear you beg for me." He tells me as he slides the head of his cock between my throbbing folds.

"Ben." I plead.

He smiles and then slams into me. Filling me completely. I nearly cry from relief. I even welcome the slight sting. He pulls back out, slowly and then thrusts back into me. The pleasure is nearly indescribable. I beg for more as he continues to plunge into me, and when I feel another tsunami building inside of me, I beg him to come with me.

He bobs his head up and down, letting me know he's there, and then he lets out a growl as he slams into me a final time, his release exploding inside of me, my core clenching around his length as my nails rake down his back and I yell out his name.

"Holy fuck." I pant as I try to catch my breath.

"Amen to that." He replies.

After our heart rates have returned to a normal state, I curl into him, resting my head on his chest. "Who knew married sex is even better than engaged sex?"

"That was pretty fucking amazing." His voice vibrating under my cheek, before he suddenly rolls me over to hover over to grin salaciously down at me. "But I'm just getting started Mrs. Sapphire."

I hope you loved Ben and Jill's story, the last installment of The Auction Series! If you did, I would be so grateful to have you leave a review. It only has to be one sentence, but it can make all the difference to our books being seen.

If you liked The Auction Series, and want a little bit more of the naughty, check out my Tempting Nights series. Each full-length book features a story about an escort from the elite Temptation Agency. Each book is a stand-alone, and each one has a happily-ever-after.
The first book is called Tempting Secrets and it's free on all platforms.
You can download it here:
https://geni.us/temptingsecrets

Acknowledgments

This book was a bit of a struggle for me, as it was a rewrite. It was previously published as Breaking Benjamin, co-written by Haylee Thorne. Haylee and I shared a special friendship at the time we wrote the original, so having to go back and change the story wasn't easy emotionally. There were aspects of the original story I just wasn't happy with though, including some of the character building, so after some thought, I asked Haylee, who is no longer actively writing, to buy the rights of the book.

I wanted to try and give the story more of my voice and I wanted it to be a continued story of the Sapphire brothers, the bond they shared, and also the struggles they both went through to finally find love. I loved writing Ben and hope I make you fall in love with him a little too.

I really want to thank Lydia Michaels for pushing me back into writing, showing me I still had what it takes to follow and conquer my dreams, and for ALWAYS having my back.

Behind the Keys Retreat girls, you know who you are; I love and respect you so much and am so thankful to have such a smart, strong group of women to call friends.

To my husband. I know I say this in every book, but you

are the reason I get to do this. When you tell me all you want is for me to be happy, you actually mean it. You support me in every way, and continue to love me in a way I never thought possible. Thank you for being my rock, my pillar of strength, the arms I can always crawl into. I love you so much more than I could ever get into words.

To my three kids. Thank you for your endless encouragement, making fun of my sex scenes, bragging about me to your friends, leaving me alone when I need it, and filling my heart with more love than I probably deserve.

Last but not least, to my readers. Thank you, thank you, thank you. Whether you've been around for awhile, (Cin Medley my biggest Sapphire fan), or are just getting started with me, you are the reason I do this. I love telling a story. And the fact that I get to keep doing this, is only because of you.

Michelle Windsor is the author of over a dozen steamy, contemporary romances filled with alpha males and even stronger females. She has achieved both Amazon and Barnes & Noble International Best Seller status, and was awarded Best Contemporary Romance Writer by Passionate Plume Ink in 2019. Her first book, The Winning Bid, was nominated for the Summit Indie Book Awards by Metamorph Publishing in 2017, and continues to be her best-selling book to date.

Michelle is married with three grown children, and lives north of Boston in the type of suburban neighborhood you read about in sweet romance books. When she's not working on another book, you can find her spending time with her husband, hanging out with her three sisters, or snuggled up with her three cats, yes three, watching a movie or reading a book.

You can find out more about Michelle, as well as links to all her books, on her webpage:
www.authormichellewindsor.com